girls who code

Team BFF:
Race to the
Finish!

by Stacia Deutsch
adapted by Christa Roberts

Penguin Workshop
An Imprint of Penguin Random House

PENGUIN WORKSHOP
Penguin Young Readers Group
An Imprint of Penguin Random House LLC

Library of Congress Cataloging-in-Publication Data is available.

ISBN 9780399542527   10 9 8 7 6 5 4 3 2 1

Hi, I'm Reshma. I'm the founder of Girls Who Code, where we teach middle- and high-school girls how to change the world by writing code and creating digital games, apps, websites, and more.

One of the most exciting things we work on—and one of my favorite topics—is robots! Robots can do all sorts of things. Girls in our program have built a robot that helps sort and recycle garbage, one that can be used as a personal assistant and provides weather, news, and music recommendations, and one that helps kids with learning disabilities. The possibilities are endless!

In this book, you'll read about Sophia and her BFFs in coding club. Together, they enter a hackathon—a marathon day of coding with other kids—and learn what it's like to code a robot. But things don't always go as planned, and they find out what it means to be there for one another—sometimes without even asking.

In addition to robots, this book is about another favorite topic of mine: sisterhood. A sisterhood is a supportive group of friends who are always there for you when you need them—it's one of the most important things we teach in our programs at Girls Who Code. Sisterhood is about working together to solve a tough problem, giving one another courage to try new things, and asking for help when you need it.

If you like what you read in this book, I hope you'll join one of our free coding clubs—and maybe even go to a hackathon and create your own robot! We're building a sisterhood of tens of thousands of girls across the country and the world—and we'd love for you to join us.

Happy reading—and coding!

Reshma Saujani

Reshma Saujani

Chapter One

"Touchdown!" I mouthed, holding my camera steadily in place. Coach Tilton pumped his fist excitedly downfield, and I let the viewfinder stay on him for a few seconds. The towering oak trees that surrounded the Halverston Middle School athletic field were just beginning to turn color, and the air was crisp and cool. Perfect football weather.

"Did you get that?" Tyson called over to me. I was in charge of filming the play from across the field, and Tyson Phillips, the other student manager, was getting the close-up.

I made sure the mic was off and adjusted the strap on my camera. "Like you even need to ask!"

We liked to compare video footage and make sure we'd gotten everything Coach wanted. People thought being a manager meant standing around, telling the players what to do, or filling the coolers with water bottles, but it was actually hard work—especially when Coach Tilton was in charge.

Tyson was lying on his stomach, getting one last shot. The football players were piling up on one another as if it were the first touchdown they'd ever scored—and this was just practice. I sprinted over to Tyson and nudged his giant foot with my sneaker as he rolled over. "Show me what you got, superstar," he said, squinting up at me.

Tyson was in ninth grade, and at first I'd been a little nervous around him. But he was really funny and down-to-earth. Sometimes I forgot he was three years older than me.

I knelt down beside him, and we quickly looked at the playback. We had to be fast if we didn't want to miss anything—or get mowed down by the players.

"Nice work, Soph," Tyson said, nodding appreciatively. "You've got a good eye."

"Thanks," I said, feeling proud.

"For a middle schooler." He winked, and I crossed my arms and sighed. I should have known he'd tease me. I didn't really mind, though. Since I was only in sixth grade, it *was* a big deal that Coach had given me the job alongside a high-school freshman. Coach usually only picked seventh- or eighth-graders to comanage the high school football team along with a high schooler. But I'd lobbied hard for it—I was curious what it'd be like to be a manager—plus, I was good at being in charge. I'd been playing sports since I was little, I was a hard worker, and I think I'd impressed Coach with my ideas for keeping the team organized. Honestly, it didn't feel that different from taking care of my three little sisters, Lola, Pearl, and Rosie. Not that I'd tell the guys that.

I shielded my eyes from the sun and looked back toward Coach as he yelled at the players to run faster. But a flash on the nearby soccer field caught my eye. A supercute, athletic, smiling kind of flash named Sammy Cooper, a boy I'd known since we crashed into each other playing soccer back in kindergarten—and who happened to be in coding club with me.

His cleat made contact with the ball, and—*whoosh!*—it sailed across the field, sending the midfielders scrambling.

"Amazing," I muttered, nodding. It wasn't easy to impress me, but Sammy had serious skills. And even though he was Focused with a capital *F*, he had a huge smile plastered on his face. I swear I never saw him *not* smiling.

Except apparently he wasn't *that* focused, because he turned and looked in my direction. Unless he also had supersonic hearing, there was no way he'd heard me compliment him, but still, I quickly averted my eyes. I didn't want him to think I was staring at him.

Because I wasn't.

Okay, maybe just a little.

I realized that my heart was thumping, and I willed it to calm down. Clearing my throat, I turned to Tyson.

"Feels like practice is going on forever today," I said.

"Yeah, Coach seems pretty set on wearing the guys out." Tyson pulled a microfiber cloth from his pocket and wiped his camera lens. It was pretty funny how obsessive he was about keeping the glass clean. "Hey, I can stay late, if you want to go," he said. "I'm gonna have to upload these videos at the computer lab, anyway—I can upload yours, too, if you want."

"You sure?" I usually felt 100 percent focused at football practice, but I was kind of preoccupied today. "Coach wants the footage tonight, Tyson. Not next year," I said with a teasing grin.

"I've gotten a lot better in the lab, Soph. I only had to call the service desk twice last time."

I raised an eyebrow.

He sighed. "Okay, fine, three times."

"You can always call me, you know," I reminded him. "One day you won't have a computer pro like me around—you should take full advantage of my genius while you can."

Tyson chuckled and nodded. "Very true." He couldn't deny that I was better at the tech side of our job.

I walked over to Coach during the next water break and took a deep breath. "Coach, I was wondering if I could—"

"Sophia." Coach cut me off, his hand on my shoulder. His voice was deep and booming—he never needed a microphone, even when players were halfway down the field. "We're going to do another practice run. I need you to take notes on what you see. You're my second set of eyes." He patted my back like he did to the players when they needed a pep talk, and then strode across the field while shouting to the quarterback, "Blake, pull back to the twenty-yard line!"

Sigh. That did *not* go like I'd hoped.

I jogged over to Tyson, who was rearranging cones. Never a break for us managers. "No luck."

"Aw, man." Tyson shook his head. "Too bad." He looked over at the players across the field. "Looks like it's gonna be a long afternoon."

I sighed. "Yep. Thanks for offering, anyway." I grabbed a scorepad and headed to the sidelines.

I could see where Coach was coming from. And it felt pretty good to know how much he relied on me. But I didn't want to be a second set of eyes. I wanted to be first in line for my mom's attention.

We'd planned a family dinner tonight, and I needed to talk to my mom before she went to work and Abuela and Pearl got home from dance class. My mom was a nurse at the hospital, so I usually didn't see her before I left for school in the morning. We texted a lot, but it wasn't the same as talking in person, and I had a LOT to tell her.

The second the football team headed to the lockers, Tyson and I scrambled to put the equipment away. The football field was always a total disaster after practices—there were football bins and cones strewn everywhere. "Yo, we got this!" one of the guys called over to me. He and another player picked up a training net and started toward the shed.

"Cool, thanks!" I answered. Usually a few of the players helped put away some of the stuff, but it was part of our job as managers to make sure the field was spotless. When training first started back in the summer, some of the guys had been pretty unhappy to see a sixth-grade student manager. I knew that I had to go out there and work as hard as Tyson. So that's what I did. And it wasn't long before I felt like the team really *did* accept me. They didn't treat me any differently than they did Tyson. And if they did ... they'd hear about it.

The equipment shed was hot and smelled like a combo of plastic, leather, and sweat. Pretty gross, but by now, we were all used to it.

"Where do these flags go again?" Tyson asked me, waving one around.

I gave him a pained look. At the beginning of the season, I'd created a detailed system (my specialty). My friends liked to call me the Queen of Organization. Honestly, it was the only way to survive in a house with three little sisters, my parents, and Abuela.

"In the bins," I directed, nodding in their direction. Seriously, the guy could recite a play-by-play of every game for the past three seasons, but give him a color-coded organization chart, and he was a lost puppy. "Balls go on the shelf, and cones in that box."

I checked my phone—my dad had given me his old one. It was kind of slow but worked for e-mails and texts. It wasn't too late. If I hurried, I might still get a chance to talk to my mom before the rest of my family got her attention.

Because once they did ... I didn't stand a chance.

■ ▄▪

"Mom!" I shouted as soon as I opened the front door. "Your favorite child is home!" I dropped my backpack by the coatrack, hung up my jacket, and took my shoes off. The smell of lime and cilantro made my stomach rumble.

"*Hola, niña!*" my mom said when I walked into the kitchen. She was wearing jeans and a T-shirt instead of her scrubs. That meant she wasn't leaving right away.

I gave her a hug. "Hi, Mom."

She hugged me back. "Your hair smells like football field grass," she said, scrunching her nose. She was chopping up avocado. "My special menu," she explained, gesturing toward the bowl of steaming basmati rice and a plate of chargrilled chicken. Mom's special menu was a way for us all to pick what we wanted, whether it was a tortilla filled with rice, chicken, and the fixings, or just rice and toppings with chips. "Want to do the chips and salsa?"

"I was hoping you'd give me a job the minute I walked in," I said, rolling my eyes. I ripped open a bag of chips and put a handful on each of our plates except Lola's. She liked to do it herself.

My mom gave me a devilish smile. "You'll get really excited later when I ask you to load the dishwasher," she said with a wink. "So what's new, sweetie?" She scooped out another avocado. "You said you had something you wanted to talk about when you texted me. How was practice?"

I thought about Sammy's rumpled soccer shirt and huge smile. Had he been looking at *me* or just in my general direction?

My mom waggled her fingers in front of my face. "Are you okay, Soph?"

"Huh?" I said, giving my head a little shake. Definitely too much Sammy on my brain. "Oh yeah, so yesterday at—"

"*Hola*, Sophia!" my grandmother bellowed as she barged into the kitchen. She wasn't a big person, but she had a way of taking up a lot of space. She and my mom had the same dark hair and bright green eyes, and they weren't that tall. People often thought they were sisters; no one ever guessed that Abuela was almost seventy years old. I had the same dark hair and take-charge attitude, but I got my height and brown eyes from my dad.

Abuela noticed the block of cheese sitting on the counter and immediately started rummaging around the cupboard for the grater. "I'm glad you saved something for me to do when I got back," she said, unwrapping the cheese. "Pearl's dance lesson ended late today. Those little girls just want to *move!*" She shimmied as she grated the cheese.

I tried not to laugh at her silly dance moves. She wore loud clothes—long, colorful ponchos and chunky jewelry—and always wanted to hear about what was going on at school. I loved her, but she could be kind of chatty, and sometimes I just wanted my mom to myself.

I emptied a jar of salsa into a bowl and was about to tell Mom all about coding club when I realized something strange: The house was eerily quiet.

"Where is everybody?" I asked, sneaking a chip and dipping it in salsa.

"Pearl's playing with her dolls in her room," Abuela said, raising her eyebrows. "The dolls are all in ballet class, and she is pretending to be their teacher."

"Dad got home early and took Rosie to the park," Mom chimed in, taking silverware out of the drawer and setting it on the counter. "And Lola's in her room, drawing." Lola spent a lot of time drawing. She was smart and creative, but she didn't always look at you when you were talking, and she got fidgety easily. My parents said she was on the autism spectrum, but she was just Lola to me: my spunky, brave, eight-year-old little sister.

"Okay, Mom, so listen," I said, taking a deep breath.

"Remember how I told you about the hackathon this weekend?" So much had happened in the last month of coding club. I hadn't been able to catch Mom up on everything.

"A hachaflon? What's that?" Abuela asked. She was from Puerto Rico, and sometimes her accent was pretty strong, especially with words she didn't know.

"Hackathon, Abuela," I corrected. "It's like a supercool marathon day of coding." I'd watched some videos of hackathons, and everyone looked so into it—focused and competitive. Plus, there were usually awesome adult coders—like mentors—to help you. That was when I knew: I, Sophia Torres, had to be a part of something like that.

"Ah, hack-a-thon," Abuela repeated slowly. Her eyebrows furrowed. "What does 'marathon day of coding' mean?"

I was glad Abuela was interested, but how do you explain computer science to someone who has trouble using the TV remote? And my time with Mom was limited.

I explained as simply as I could. "You know how I mentioned coding club to you?" Abuela nodded. "Well, the hackathon is an event this Saturday at the community center that I'm going to with my friends from coding club. We have to come up with a coding project, and there'll be kids from other schools there, too."

Mrs. Clark had told us that if one of the teams from our coding club got the top prize, she would take them out for ice cream. We'd been super excited about the hackathon, anyway, but now we wanted to do it even more. Plus, Sammy's team was going to be there, too, and I couldn't let them get a prize and not us.

"Sounds great, sweetie," Mom replied, but I wasn't sure she was really listening—she was warming tortillas in the oven, and the buzzer was ringing. "I wonder if they're warm enough," she said to herself, peering in the oven.

"*Sí*, sounds fun!" Abuela said, but I knew she had no idea what I was talking about. She glanced over at my mom and the oven. "Another minute, *m'ija*."

"Mom!" I snapped my fingers. "This is important!"

Abuela made a clicking sound with her tongue. "*Tsk.* Do not snap the fingers at your mama, Sophia. Very disrespectful."

I blew out my breath. "Sorry." I sat down at one of the stools at our small kitchen island. "Mrs. Clark asked us all to sign up for the hackathon at coding club last week," I said, thinking about how when Mrs. Clark brought in the permission forms, my friend Lucy had the biggest smile I'd ever seen from her, and that's saying a lot—Lucy Morrison was the bubbliest person I knew. "My coding group is going as a team. Dad filled out the paperwork."

"Great, honey." Mom took the tortilla platter out of the oven and put it on the kitchen table. "Who's in your group again?"

"Lucy; Maya Chung; and the new girl, Erin Roberts—you know, the seventh-grader who moved here this year." I thought about how Mrs. Clark had decided the four of us should be a "permanent group" after the first week of coding club because we worked so well together. We'd become close outside coding club, too, and I couldn't imagine school without them now.

Mom patted my hand. "I'm so happy you and Lucy are getting along again, Soph."

"Yeah, me too." Lucy and I had been BFFs for years, but we'd drifted apart last year when I thought she didn't want to be friends anymore. Turned out it was a big misunderstanding, and now we were BFFs again.

"So, anyway," I went on. "First we have to come up with a plan for what to code at the hackathon, so my friends are coming over later to work on it."

"That's fine, Sophia," Mom said. She gave me a stern look. "But in the future, you should ask me first before you invite people over." Abuela was nodding behind her. I didn't like having them gang up on me.

"I *tried*, Mom, but you were busy." The words rushed out before I could stop them. I gave my mom my best *don't-be-mad-at-me* face. "But next time I'll ask."

My mom's expression relaxed. "I *am* glad you're enjoying the club."

"Me too," I said, sitting down at the table.

Abuela walked over to the stairs. "Pearl, Lola—dinnertime!"

I crunched on a chip. "You'll be able to come to the hackathon, right, Mom? Mrs. Clark said parents can come at the end to see our coding projects." Mom had been busy with my little sisters these days and had missed the last three football games I'd helped oversee. I didn't usually mind, but I really hoped she could be at the hackathon. We were working hard, and I wanted her to see how cool coding was.

"I'd love to, sweetie. I'll check my schedule."

Boom! Boom! Boom! My sisters sounded like a herd of elephants running down the stairs. Pearl came in first, throwing herself into Mom's arms. She was little but fast. "Mama! Watch!" She spun around in a circle. "See how good I dance?"

"Amazing," my mom gushed, clapping. "But it's time for dinner, sweet pea."

Pearl took her usual seat at the table, next to Abuela. She was still wearing her pink leotard, and her curly long hair was pulled back in a ponytail. "I'm going to put on a show for you tonight, Abuela," she said, wiggling back and forth.

Abuela winked. "I can't wait to see it, *mi amor*. Now, here, have some rice," she urged, putting a big spoonful on her plate. My sisters went to bed early, so they started eating right away while Mom finished getting things ready.

Lola was usually pretty quiet unless she was talking about her favorite subject: dogs. Once she started telling you about them, she'd go on forever. She was already sitting down, looking out the kitchen window. "Daddy!" she burst out suddenly.

Two seconds later, the door that led to the garage opened, and my dad entered with my youngest sister, two-year-old Rosie, toddling beside him.

"Sophia!" Rosie shouted, half running to me. She wrapped her little arms around my neck. "Missed you!"

"I missed you, too," I said, kissing her pink cheeks and tickling her tummy as she giggled.

"Perfect timing," Mom said, filling the girls' cups with milk. "Everything's ready."

Dad gave Lola and me each a peck on top of our heads.

"How're my girls?" he asked, mussing up my hair.

"Hungry," I declared. Mom liked for us to wait until everyone was at the table before we said grace, but the food just smelled so good, I couldn't help myself. I piled a tortilla with chicken, cheese, avocado, and salsa, rolled it up, and took a huge bite.

Dad chuckled. "Looks like you weren't kidding, Soph." He leaned in to give Mom a quick kiss.

"Yuck!" Lola put a hand over her eyes. "Gross!"

"Someday you'll like kisses." Mom made a loud *smooch*ing sound. "Someday you might even want to give one to someone."

"Ewww!" Lola and Pearl shrieked together, and Lola stuck out her tongue in disgust.

A few minutes later, everyone was finally sitting together at the table. It was a typical dinner at Casa Torres. Rosie was dropping shredded cheese all over the floor. Pearl was talking about ballet class with her mouth open. Abuela was trying to coax Lola into eating more chicken, and Mom and Dad were eating and chatting about work.

I took another bite of my burrito and frowned. My friends would be here soon, and my one-on-one time with Mom had disappeared as fast as the warm tortillas.

"Chip, pwease!" Rosie said, raising both her hands.

Sighing, I put one chip on her plate and three on mine.

"You can have another one if you don't drop it," I told her. She stuck out her bottom lip. "Okay, fine," I said, giving her two more chips. She grinned, and I smiled back at her. On the bright side, at least I *had* been able to tell my mom about the hackathon. And when she came to see it, I could finally show her what coding club was all about!

We had just finished dinner when Pearl started yawning, Lola spilled her milk, and Rosie put her head down on the table.

"The girls are exhausted," Mom said, getting up. "I'll take them up and get them ready for their baths."

Abuela rose, too. "I will help, *m'ija*, so you can get to work on time."

Mom gave her a grateful look. Mom scooped up Rosie from her chair and kissed the top of her head. "Who's ready for some bubbles?"

"*Vamos, chiquitas!*" Abuela commanded as she herded Lola and Pearl out of the kitchen.

Dad carried his dinner plate to the sink and sighed. "Those girls," he said, shaking his head. "It's nonstop energy, isn't it?" It was amazing how quiet it got once my sisters, Mom, and Abuela left the room.

"Yeah," I agreed, enjoying the calm.

"Music?" Dad asked me, turning on the old-school radio we had on the counter.

I grinned. "Only if we play what I like."

He found my favorite pop station, and we hummed along to the song. We were halfway through loading the dishwasher when the doorbell rang.

Dad's forehead wrinkled. "I wonder who that is, this time of night." He glanced at his watch. "Probably someone selling something."

"Yeah," I said. Then, suddenly, I remembered my plans. "Oh! It's my friends!"

Dad raised an eyebrow. "On a school night?"

"We're not just hanging out, Dad, we're working on something for coding club. I told Mom they were coming, and she said it was fine."

"Okay, go ahead," he said, putting the silverware in the cutlery basket. "I'll take care of the rest."

"Thanks, Dad!" I exclaimed, rushing to the door.

Ring ring

Ring ring ring

Ring ring ring ring

There was only one person impatient enough to ring the bell that many times.

Chapter Two

"Hi!" Lucy said excitedly when I opened the door. She gave me a wave instead of ringing the bell again. Maya and Erin were standing next to her.

Lucy's black hair was pulled back into two neat, tight braids, and she had on her bright heart-shaped stud earrings, which stood out against her dark skin. She'd been wearing those a lot lately—I was pretty sure it was because Maya had told her they looked cute.

"Hey," Maya said, making her way into the house. If Lucy was a trend chaser, Maya was most definitely a trendsetter. She was wearing black drawstring pants matched with a loose floral top. I was amazed at how she could make anything fashionable, even something I thought looked like pajamas.

"I brought treats." Erin tapped her paisley-print

backpack. "Homemade s'mores cookies."

"Yum!" I said, ushering my friends in. Everyone took off their shoes and hung their coats on the coatrack.

"Lucy, did you bring the binder?" I asked. Over the last week, Lucy and I had organized everything we'd learned in coding club into a white two-inch binder to help us get ready for the hackathon, and we'd included all the information about the hackathon, too. It was nice to have a best friend who loved organizing things as much as I did.

"The binder?" Lucy gasped, dramatically putting her hand on her chest. "I had *one* job. How could I have forgotten?"

I rolled my eyes. "Never mind. I see it in your bag, Lu."

She dropped her hand and giggled. "You only texted me about a million times to remember it, Soph."

My dad popped out of the kitchen to say hello to my friends, and we then headed toward my room.

"I'm so bummed I missed coding club yesterday," Maya grumbled, making a face. "What did you do?"

"Wait, first tell us what happened at the dance meeting," Erin said as we trooped upstairs. "I thought you were going to text us about it." As president of the student council, Maya was in charge of organizing the upcoming winter dance at school. They'd had their first meeting yesterday during coding club, which was why she'd missed it.

"Ugh, my battery died last night, and I couldn't find my charger." Maya groaned.

"Not being able to find things . . . welcome to the story of my life," Erin said, shaking her head. "I lost my glasses yesterday, and you'll never guess where I found them."

"Your backpack?" Lucy ventured.

Erin giggled as she tapped her lens. "Nope. On my face!"

We all laughed as we walked into my bedroom.

"I wouldn't have wanted to text you about the meeting, anyway," Maya said, plopping onto my bed and sighing.

"Why?" I asked. "I thought you were so excited about it."

"I *was*," Maya explained. "Until I got there and hardly anybody showed up! Some people were out sick, and I guess other people just forgot or something. And our advisor was super late, so basically nothing happened."

Lucy spread out on the floor and pulled the binder from her bag. "Did you talk about the theme? Or decorations?"

"Nope," Maya said, shaking her head. "It was super annoying. When I saw how many people were missing,

I should have just canceled the meeting and gone to coding club instead."

Erin offered Maya a cookie. "Here, have a s'more. Maybe it'll make you feel better."

Maya shrugged. "One will make me feel a *little* better." She reached into the tin. "Two would make me feel a *lot* better!"

I went over to grab a cookie, too. They had a graham cracker crust with melted chocolate and roasted mini marshmallows on top. I licked my lips and took a bite, making sure not to get any crumbs on my floor. "Mmm . . . so good, Erin!"

I took a seat at my desk. "Okay, so we need to talk about our plan for the hackathon," I said. I pulled out a small whiteboard from behind my desk and erased last week's predictions. My dad and I always wrote down our forecasts before we watched football games together. I had totally beaten him last weekend—as usual.

Maya rummaged through her bag. "Gahhh, here it is." She held up her charger and waved it around. Then she took out her sketchbook—we hardly ever saw her without it. "Did Mrs. Clark tell you more about the hackathon yesterday?" she asked.

Lucy clapped. "Oh, we have to tell Maya the theme!"

Maya raised an eyebrow. "We couldn't even come up

with a theme for the dance, but you're telling me there's one for the hackathon?"

Lucy nodded. "Yes." She paused dramatically. "The theme is . . . *robots*!"

"Beep beep bop!" Erin playfully imitated robot sounds, moving her arms around stiffly. "Beep bop boop!" Erin loved acting, and she was really good at voices. And apparently, at robots, too.

Lucy started bumping into Maya, saying, "Error! Error!"

Erin lifted her arms and twisted her upper body to the left, keeping her back straight. She moved mechanically, a blank expression on her face.

Lucy and Maya couldn't stop giggling. "She's doing the robot!" Maya said, clapping.

Lucy clutched her neck with one hand and her leg with her other hand and began hopping up and down. "Watch out, Sophia, or you're going to get wet. It's spuh-rinkler time!"

Suddenly my bedroom had turned into a full-on dance party. Maya hopped off my bed and pretended she was pushing a shopping cart around. She guided the "cart" between Erin and Lucy, who squealed and moved out of the way. Reaching up toward my bedroom walls, she grabbed and tossed imaginary items into the pretend cart.

I tried hard not to laugh. "Stop goofing around, guys!" But my friends wouldn't listen. Lucy stopped being a sprinkler for a second to grab my hand and pull me up. "Come on, Soph, show us your moves!"

I crossed my arms, feeling a flare of annoyance in my chest. We were supposed to be coding, not dancing! But to be honest, the empty expression on Erin's "robot" face *was* pretty hilarious. I broke into my best running man shuffle as my BFFs egged me on.

"We look ridiculous," Lucy gasped, doubled over laughing.

"Speak for yourself," I panted, hopping in place and swinging my arms.

Before long, we were all rolling on the floor in hysterics.

Across the room, I heard my phone vibrate. I disentangled myself from my friends and picked it up. It was probably Abuela practicing texting again—she kept sending me texts that said "TEST" (yes, in caps. Don't ask). I'd write her back, and then she'd say she couldn't find the texting app. Typical. But when I saw who the text was from, my heart skipped a beat.

"Ooh, you're turning red, Sophia!" Maya said, looking at me with a curious expression. "Did you get a text from a secret admirer?"

My cheeks felt hot, and I hoped my face hadn't turned

beet red. "What? No, it's nothing."

Lucy came up behind me and peered over my shoulder. "By 'nothing' she means she got a text from Sammy and it says, 'See you tomorrow.'" She gave me an incredulous look. "Sammy, like Sammy Cooper from coding club? Why is he texting you?" Her brown eyes opened wide. "Ooh, is *this* what you were talking about the other day?"

"No, it's not! It's nothing," I said a little too loudly, quickly turning my phone off. Sammy and I were in English class together, and he'd been out last Friday, so he asked me about what he'd missed. We'd exchanged numbers, and he'd texted me a few times. I hadn't told my friends, though Lucy had pried out of me that *maybe* I had a crush on somebody.

"Talking about what the other day?" Erin asked, rolling onto her stomach and propping herself up on her elbows. "Sounds mysterious."

I shoved my phone into my desk drawer, grabbed my whiteboard, and sat down at my desk. "I swear, it's nothing. Hackathon, remember?" I crossed my legs and gave my friends my best no-nonsense face, hoping my cheeks weren't still flushed. "So, we need robot ideas."

"I bet Sammy would be happy to help you brainstorm ideas," Lucy said slyly.

Erin made smooching sounds. "Oh, Sophia. I had a question about algorithms, and it just can't wait until school tomorrow," she said dreamily, batting her eyelashes.

Maya started giggling. "Somebody has a cru-ush," she said in a singsongy voice.

I kept my expression blank. "When you're done amusing yourselves, just let me know."

The three of them gave a collective sigh. "Maybe you need another s'more," Erin said, pushing the tin toward me.

I scowled in her direction. "Bribes will get you nowhere." But I did reach for another cookie. "Are we ready?"

"Ooooooookeydoke." Lucy picked up the binder and started paging through it. "Mrs. Clark told us that each team will get what they need for a programmable robot: a robot rover, which is like the base of the robot, and a motherboard."

"What's a motherboard?" Maya asked.

Erin broke off a chunk of cookie. "It's like the command center for the robot. The rover has four wheels and a flat thing on it, and the motherboard goes on top, right?"

Lucy nodded. "That's what we connect to the computer to program it. Look, like this." She turned the binder toward us and showed us an image we'd printed out of a metal rectangle on wheels with another metal piece on top of it.

We all leaned in to take a look.

"And we'll have to add modules to it, I think?" Erin chimed in.

I remembered that part from yesterday. "Yeah. There'll be things like lights and movable arms that we can add to our robot rover—it should have four slots where we can plug them in."

"And there'll be a table of supplies where we can get other stuff like balls, blocks, or string," Lucy added. "Basically any four modules we want to add to our robot."

Maya flipped through the pages we'd printed about modules. "Cool, but does the robot have to do something? Or do we just add modules for fun?"

"I think it does have to do something," Lucy said, pressing her lips together and squinting thoughtfully. "Hang on." She flipped through the binder to the hackathon information sheet that Mrs. Clark had given us, and read:

> *You will code your robot to go through the judges'*
> *maze. The maze will be a six-foot square. It will have*
> *low walls and dead ends that the robots will have*
> *to get around to reach the exit. It's not just about*

finishing first, though—prizes will be awarded for creativity, coding, and the most imaginative robot.

Maya nibbled on her fingernail. "So we have to get our robot to go through a maze, *and* it has to be super creative? What does that even mean?"

We were all stumped when there was a knock on my door.

"Come in!" I called out, glad for the distraction.

My mom poked her head in. "Hey, girls," she said, smiling at my friends. She had changed out of her jeans and into her scrubs. "I hate to interrupt, Sophia, but I'm leaving soon, and I had a quick question."

Behind her, I could hear voices echoing down the hallway.

"Clean teeth are important!" Abuela was saying, probably to Pearl.

Mom glanced back into the hall. "When's the hackathon again?" she asked me.

"Saturday," I told her, feeling a little exasperated. Was it *that* hard to remember?

"Right . . ." Mom nodded slowly. "Okay, I'll talk to Dad about it." Then she gave me a kiss. "See you tomorrow, honey," she said, closing the door.

"Does your mom work every night?" Erin asked.

"No. Her schedule changes," I explained. "Sometimes

she works days, sometimes she works nights—it all depends on how busy the hospital is."

"You two have the same smile," Maya remarked, looking up from her sketchbook. She had started doodling a robot with swirly designs all over it.

"Yeah," I said, looking down at my whiteboard. I had a sinking feeling in my stomach. My mom was going to miss yet *another* one of my events. I could just feel it.

Maya waved her sketchbook around. "Earth to Sophia!"

I tried to shake off my bad feeling. "Sorry." I straightened my whiteboard on my lap. "So, we need to figure out how to get our robot through the maze."

"*And* be creative," Lucy added, sounding hopeless.

The only sound was Maya's pencil on her sketchpad.

Lucy raised a finger. "Didn't Mrs. Clark talk about how we should plan out our robot idea?"

I nodded. "Yeah. She talked about coming up with the idea, planning the algorithm, and then coding the algorithm." I wrote down the three steps on my whiteboard in separate columns.

Maya looked up from her pad and gave my whiteboard a dismissive look. "Can't we just, like, code the robot when we get there?"

"No, we can't," I said, getting annoyed. I actually liked

the steps Mrs. Clark had described. It gave us a clear plan—Coach Tilton would have approved. "We have to figure everything out ahead of time so that we know what to do when we get to the coding part," I explained. Lucy and Erin nodded.

Maya was fiddling with her choker. "Okay, I get the 'idea' part, but what's the algorithm part?"

"An algorithm is a set of instructions a computer follows in a certain order to complete a task," Lucy said. "Mrs. Clark talked about it at the meeting you missed."

Erin sat up and crossed her legs. "Exactly. I think what we need to do is plan our algorithm with pseudocode."

"Pseudowhat?" Maya asked.

"Pseudocode is code that humans can read and computers can't, remember?"

"Oh yeah. But that's useful how?" I said. "Since we're, um, working with a robot?"

Erin thought for a minute. "You know how Coach Tilton writes up directions for players?"

I frowned. "You mean, the plays?"

Erin beamed like I'd just given her a gold star. "Yeah! The plays. Well, pseudocode is kind of like that. You have to write down the logic of your code to help you plan before you write the code."

"Just like the players need a game plan before they run onto the field and start tackling people," Lucy said, catching on.

"Wait." Maya leaned over to grab Lucy's wrist. "Is that a Rudolf Randolf wrap bracelet?"

I hadn't noticed the woven blue silk cord that was wrapped several times around Lucy's wrist.

"Yeah." Lucy grinned. "A client of my mom's gave it to her as a thank-you gift for solving some big computer problem. Mom said it wasn't her style, so she let me have it." Lucy moved her arm so everyone could see how the royal blue shimmered against her dark skin. Her mom was a software programmer—one of the only black female coders at her company. "Isn't it cool?" Lucy wasn't as into fashion as Maya was, but she liked adding little touches to her outfits.

Maya ran her fingers over the cord. "I love it. Can I borrow it sometime?"

"Sure." Lucy beamed.

"It's superspecial that you're sharing your jewelry and all, but can we focus?" I said, rapping my knuckles on the whiteboard. If I didn't keep us on task, no one would. "We have a hackathon to plan for, remember?"

"Yes, Coach Sophia," Maya said, saluting me.

We all giggled and got back to our robot plan.

Maya tapped her eraser against her mouth. "So if we figure all this out now, we can bring notes to the hackathon, right?" She started doodling again. "'Cause there's no way I'm gonna remember all of this."

"No notes." I looked at Lucy and Erin. "Didn't Mrs. Clark say that?"

Lucy nodded. "And we can't really practice beforehand, since we don't have the robot or modules. I think we just have to come up with an idea for what we want our robot to do and hope we can make it happen at the hackathon."

It seemed impossible. Even though we'd learned a lot in coding club over the past few months, none of us had ever coded a robot before.

We finished all the s'mores and tried to come up with ideas for how to get our robot through the maze (*and* be original at the same time). But we were losing steam—Lucy couldn't stop yawning, and Maya kept drawing.

Suddenly Erin stood up and started playing music from her phone. Loud music.

I looked at her. "Um, Erin, what are you doing?" We were all getting tired, but now wasn't the time for music. It was kind of frustrating that she wasn't taking this more seriously.

"What does it look like I'm doing?" she said, shaking her hips. "Dancing!"

"Again?" I groaned. "If you're even thinking about doing the worm—"

Maya tilted her head. "Wait, what's this song? Erin . . . is that *you* singing?"

Erin grinned. "Do you like it?"

"Oh my gosh, it *is* you!" I said, recognizing her voice. The song was fast and upbeat, but Erin's voice was soft and melodic.

"It's this song called 'Dance to the Beat' that we're doing for film club. They're going to film me dancing, so I need to practice." She reached for Maya's hand.

"Maybe our robot could play 'Dance to the Beat'!" Erin said, spinning Maya around.

One of the modules they'd provide at the hackathon was a speaker, so it *could* work. I wrote "Play 'Dance to the Beat'" in the Ideas column on the board.

"Any other modules we should try to use?" Lucy asked.

I considered the list. An arm and a ball—if the robot could be musical like Erin, couldn't it be sporty, too?

"Maybe we could have the robot push one of the balls," I suggested.

Lucy came over to look at the pages with me. "That

could be cool. I doubt anyone else will do that."

An image of Sammy kicking the soccer ball floated into my mind. He might think of this idea, too. Still, I wrote "Push the ball" under Ideas on the whiteboard.

Maya leaned down to look at the open page of the binder. "Maybe we could combine the ball with something else."

That sounded good, but I had no idea what.

"How about dancing?" Erin suggested excitedly. "I could teach our robot a few moves!" She shook her hips. "Let the algo-rhythm move you!"

"Erin, we need *serious* ideas," I said, sighing. "We want to win this thing, don't we?" I asked.

Maya wagged her eyebrows. "Yeah . . . but I think *you* have a little extra motivation."

I frowned. "Like what?"

"Oh nothing . . . ," Erin trilled, sashaying across the room. Then she turned around dramatically. "Like beating Sammy!"

"Whatever," I said dismissively. "*Of course* I want to beat him. I want to beat *everybody*!"

"Uh-huh," Erin answered, shaking her hips.

Lucy was the only one who seemed to be focusing on our coding project. "Soph, any idea is a good idea, right?" That's what Mrs. Clark always said. "I think you should write Erin's idea down."

I wrote "Dancing," even though it was obviously impossible. The rover looked like a car, not a ballerina. "Anything else?"

No one could come up with more ideas. "We've done enough work. DJ Erin says it's time to boogie!" Erin said, dropping her voice. She turned up the music and started spinning around.

"Friends don't let friends dance alone," Lucy shouted, joining in. And that was how our coding club meeting ended with the four of us dancing around my room like maniacs. Again.

Before my friends left, I remembered one more thing.

"Maya, wait, I have to give you your T-shirt." I handed her one of the tees that Mrs. Clark had given us for the hackathon.

"Um, thanks . . ." Maya held it up. The T-shirt was white with bold yellow letters on the front that said HACKATHON. Maya wrinkled her nose like it was a slice of moldy pizza. "Do we *have* to wear this?"

I shrugged. "Mrs. Clark said we could make up a team name and decorate it if we wanted to. But we don't have to."

Maya looked relieved. She tapped her finger on her chin. "Wait, I have an idea," she said. "How about we call ourselves *the Rockin' Robots*?"

"Oh my gosh, that's perfect!" Lucy gushed, clapping. After the dance party we'd just had, it did seem fitting.

Maya looked at the T-shirt again. "Can everybody meet tomorrow after school?" We all nodded. "Awesome. Bring your T-shirts. I have tons of supplies. We have *got* to make these more presentable."

Everybody grabbed their stuff and headed downstairs. I loved hanging out with my BFFs, but we needed to come up with an original robot idea, and they seemed more interested in looking at bracelets, bugging me about Sammy, and dancing. And there were only four days until the hackathon. I just hoped we'd get it together in time—'cause there was no way I was letting Sammy's team beat us to a prize.

Chapter Three

The next day, I found Coach between classes. When he wasn't on the field, he was teaching eighth-grade English.

"Hi, Coach," I said, jogging up to him. "Sorry to ask you this, but . . . would it be okay if I missed practice this afternoon?"

He frowned. "Sophia, I gave you the manager job because you're usually so responsible."

"I know . . . and I am." I paused, giving him an apologetic look. "But I'm in coding club, and we're getting ready for our first hackathon this weekend. It's just that I need to meet with my team to prepare."

He gave me a long look. "If it's for a school-related activity, it's fine to miss practice today, Sophia." Coach pointed his finger at me, his face stern. "But don't make a habit of it."

"Thanks, Coach—I won't!" I said, running off to class.

When the last bell rang, Maya, Erin, Lucy, and I met up in front of the school to go to Maya's.

"Want to stop at the Bakeshop first?" Maya asked us. "We don't have any good snacks at my house, and I'm dying for a cake pop." Her mom was pretty strict about eating between meals, though she sometimes baked us a Chinese dessert called a sweetheart cake that was out of this world. It was a flaky pastry with a delicious spiced filling that tasted like melon and almonds.

"Hmmm, I'm not sure," Lucy said, her dark eyes twinkling. "Cinnamon buns, muffins . . . sounds *awful*."

"Right? And what if there's biscotti and apple crumb cake?" Erin gave a mock shiver. "The things we do for coding."

"All I can say is, my brain works better after a cupcake," I declared, linking my arm with Lucy's. Lucy linked hers with Erin's, and Erin joined arms with Maya, and we made our way down the street.

As soon as we walked into the Bakeshop, we realized we weren't the only ones with the same idea. We got on line, and I recognized kids from school hanging out on the couches and chairs in the main area. Out of the corner of my eye, I saw Sammy sitting with his hackathon team.

He glanced at me, and I felt my face start to get warm. It's not like I always felt awkward around boys. I spent enough time with the boys' football team to know that it was ridiculous to get nervous around them—they were loud, weird, funny, and, let's be honest, stinky. Plus, I'd known Sammy forever. But lately, I'd been getting strangely nervous around him. It's like I suddenly realized that he had the nicest smile, the deepest, brownest eyes that matched his dark skin, and the thickest, longest eyelashes I'd ever seen. I looked over again, and he gave me a wave. I turned around, my face on fire.

Lucy must have noticed, because she nudged my arm. "Sophia, wave back!" she whispered.

I gave Sammy sort of a half wave, wrist flippy thing, and then looked at the menu on the wall as if it were the most fascinating thing I'd ever seen.

Lucy leaned into me. "Maybe next time you'll actually make eye contact."

"Shut up!" I hissed, still staring at the menu, wondering what shade of red my face had become.

In front of us in line, I saw Leila, another girl from coding club. Glad for the distraction, I tapped her on the back. "Hey, Leila!"

Leila turned around and smiled. "Oh, hi, guys." A taller girl was standing next to her. "This is my sister, Tania," Leila introduced us. They both wore head scarves—Leila's was maroon, which complemented her blue eyes well, and her sister's was teal with a gold border.

Erin tucked a strand of blond hair under her slouchy gray beanie. "How's it going with your hackathon team? You're with Mark and Maddie, right?"

Their group was the only three-person team; everybody else was in teams of four or five.

Leila frowned. "Not anymore—I'm not going to the hackathon."

"Huh?" I said. That was a surprise. "Why not? It's going to be so fun." Leila seemed really into coding. She was always talking about robots, and I'd heard her say she wanted to work in artificial intelligence someday. I wasn't sure what that was, exactly, but it sounded cool.

"Mark and Maddie's grandfather died, so they won't be here for the rest of the week," Leila explained. "I just found out today. They're not coming back till Sunday."

"Oh, wow." I didn't know what to say.

"That's too bad," Maya chimed in as we inched forward in line.

Leila's sister was ordering her drink, and it was Leila's

turn now. "Yeah. It's okay—there'll be other hackathons. See you later!"

I wasn't so sure about that—I hadn't heard of that many hackathons. But the smell of chocolate distracted me. We were up next and all ordered the same thing: hot chocolate with homemade marshmallows, and we each got a snack to go with it. A group of people were getting up from a booth near the door, so we grabbed it.

"Mmmm . . . I could drink this every day," Maya said, wrapping her hands around the steaming mug of cocoa. "It. Is. So. Good."

I nodded, taking a sip. It made my stomach warm and tingly . . . or was that because of Sammy? I squeezed my eyes shut for a second, trying not to think about him. I made a mental note to pretend Sammy was Tyson next time I saw him—maybe then I wouldn't act so awkward.

"You know what I was thinking?" Erin said, spooning up a marshmallow. "Wouldn't it be cool to have a robot baking assistant? To get ingredients for you and be a mixer and stuff?"

"A girl can dream," Lucy agreed, sighing.

"Some girls are already dreaming," Maya teased, jabbing her finger into my shoulder. "About a certain soccer-playing, always-smiling—"

"Be quiet!" I hissed, holding up my palm to cut her off before she could say you-know-who's name. "For your information, I wasn't dreaming. I was thinking." Something genius had just occurred to me. "Why don't we ask Leila to join our team?" I said as I took a bite of my berry muffin.

My friends all looked at me. "That's a great idea!" Lucy exclaimed.

"Right? She seems cool, and it's not like we've come up with an amazing robot idea yet." They all nodded. "Leila's always talking about robots in coding club—maybe she could help us."

Erin nudged me. "Um, Soph? You have a hot chocolate mustache," she said quietly. "Might wanna . . ." She gestured toward her napkin.

I quickly grabbed a napkin and wiped my lips. That was the *last* thing I needed Sammy to see.

Lucy looked over in his direction. "Don't worry, he's not looking."

"*You* stop looking!" I said, elbowing her. I glanced surreptitiously across the coffee shop, and I could have sworn I saw Sammy watching me.

"Didn't Mrs. Clark say we had until this Thursday at 1:00 p.m. to sign up online for the hackathon?" I added, wanting to change the subject—fast.

"She did," Lucy answered, biting off a piece of her chocolate chip cookie. "But if we're going to invite Leila, we should probably do it now—I think Mrs. Clark also said something about not being able to change your team after signing up."

Erin polished off her cinnamon crunch muffin and crumpled the brown wrapper into a ball. "Yeah, she mentioned being disqualified. I wonder why they have such strict rules. Seems kind of weird."

"Maybe it's because they need to know how many robots and modules to get or something." Maya picked leftover chocolate off her cake-pop stick. "But I totally think we should ask Leila to join our team."

We all looked at one another and grinned.

We picked up our mugs and what was left of our snacks and walked over to Leila and her sister.

"Hi, ladies," Lucy said, sitting down at one of the empty seats at their table. She wasn't one to wait for permission.

Neither was I, so I joined her. "We have something we wanted to ask you," I began.

Leila seemed interested. "Sure. What's up?"

"We were thinking, do you want to be on our team for the hackathon?" Maya asked, looking from Leila to all of us.

Leila looked at us excitedly. "Really? You want me in your group?" she asked, her eyes lighting up.

"Totally!" I answered as my friends nodded enthusiastically. "Honestly, we could use your robot knowledge. Plus, it'd be fun to hang out!"

"And you don't want to miss it," Erin added. "It's supposed to be really fun . . . like a carnival with tons of food and activities."

"And coding," Lucy said.

Leila looked over at her sister, who smiled reassuringly back at her.

"Well, sure, why not!" Leila said.

Lucy gave her a hug. "Yay! Welcome to the Rockin' Robots!"

"Thanks so much!" Leila said, her smile ear to ear. Maya hugged her, too. "Do you have your hackathon T-shirt with you? We were going to go over to my house and paint them. You can join us, if you want."

"Let me see if I still have my T-shirt in here . . ." She rummaged through her backpack and pulled it out triumphantly.

"Awesome! Let's go—we've got some shirts to decorate!" Maya said, leading the way.

Chapter Four

When I got home that night, I was exhausted. On our shirts we'd each painted a robot that Maya had sketched out—it had a big round snowman-like head; a chunky body; two accordion arms; and two stiff, straight legs. It actually looked pretty funny. We'd used orange and gray paint—our school colors—and had written *The Rockin' Robots* on the back in chunky black puffy paint. I'd never used paint like that, but Maya was an expert. She showed us how you had to hold a steam iron above the dried paint on the hottest setting to make the paint puff up.

Maya's mom had grilled us cheeseburgers and made a yummy tomato and corn salad for dinner. While we ate, Leila told us about how she had a little brother (in addition to her sister), and how they'd moved to town from Pakistan a few years ago. Her sister was planning on going back there after college—she wanted to start a company that made robots to help farmers. Apparently, they could do things like water soil and pick plants. I had no idea robots could do that, and it got me thinking about robots to help us at football practice. It'd be pretty cool to have a robot fill footballs with air (my least favorite job, since the machine broke down all the time) or pick up footballs that had been thrown far afield. I made a mental note to talk to Coach about that.

I was in the kitchen getting a drink when Dad walked in. He was looking at his phone distractedly. "Hi, Soph. Good day at school?"

"Yeah," I answered, sipping my water.

"When did you say the hackathon was again?" he said, still glued to his phone.

I tried not to sigh. "Saturday." It was like my parents had amnesia about any of my plans but always remembered my sisters' perfectly.

"Hmm." His forehead wrinkled.

"Why?" I asked.

"Just checking," he replied, but he was still looking at his phone, and I could tell he wasn't really focused.

Normally I wouldn't just let it drop, but he was

preoccupied—and I was tired—so I put my glass in the sink and headed upstairs. That's when I heard the shouting.

I recognized Pearl's screaming right away. Even though she was only five, she had a voice that rivaled Coach Tilton's.

"Noooo!" she was yelling at the top of her lungs.

"*Pobrecita*," Abuela's soft, calm tones answered her. "Poor little girl."

I couldn't hear the problem or response, but Pearl was clearly upset. I wondered what it was this time—maybe she couldn't find her favorite teddy bear or her socks didn't match. I swear, five-year-olds got upset about the weirdest things.

"Sophia!" Dad yelled from the kitchen. "Mom got called in for an emergency tonight. I've got to finish a work thing . . . Can you help Abuela?"

I sighed. It wasn't exactly how I had wanted to spend my evening, but I was used to it. "Got it!" I called out. I dropped my backpack with a thud in my room and headed into Pearl and Rosie's bedroom.

"Whoa!" I gasped at the mess. There were clothes strewn everywhere and books on the floor. In the middle of it all, Pearl was flopped facedown, having a full-blown temper tantrum.

"She wants to wear her leotard to bed," Abuela explained to me, hands on her hips. "But she wore it all day." I remembered that today was Pearl's second dance class, and I knew how excited she'd been about it. The class must have gone well, seeing as she refused to change out of her leotard.

"I told her that ballerinas *dance* in leotards. They do not *sleep* in leotards." Abuela sighed. "I'm supposed to call Marissa in a few minutes," she went on, tapping the gold bangle watch on her wrist. Marissa was Abuela's older sister who lived in a senior citizen complex an hour away from us.

"Go call her, Abuela. I've got this," I told her firmly. "Where are Lola and Rosie?"

Abuela took a long breath. "Lola is watching a documentary about German shepherds, and Rosie got tired of Pearl's screaming. Who can blame her? She's waiting for me to read her a bedtime story in Lola's room." She pointed at Pearl, who'd stopped sobbing but refused to get up off the floor. "This little one . . . *ay dios mío*."

I plopped down next to Pearl and put a soothing hand on her back.

"Pearlie Girlie," I said, using my nickname for her. Abuela blew me a kiss and tiptoed out the door. "Did you have fun at ballet class today?"

Pearl looked up at me with a tearstained face and nodded. "So, so, so much fun," she said, choking back sniffles.

"That's great," I said gently. "But you need to change for bed now."

Pearl's eyes welled, then scrunched together. "I'm not taking off my leotard!" she said, hiccupping.

I tried not to laugh. Her little face crumpled, and she looked so determined. She was a lot like me, actually. So I knew exactly how to get her to do what I wanted.

"Okay, sure. I'm going to put on my pajamas," I began, standing up. "I just thought it would be cool if we both had on our pj's and had a little dance party before you go to bed. I was hoping you could teach me what you learned." I shrugged. "But if you don't want to . . ."

Pearl looked up at me, her eyes wide. "Wait!" And just like that, her tears were gone.

A few minutes later we were both in our pajamas. By the time Dad came upstairs, Abuela and Rosie had read together, and everything was under control. Pearl showed us some turns and kicks that didn't look exactly ballerina-like but, I had to admit, were pretty adorable. We cracked up when she spun so fast, she got dizzy and toppled into Rosie.

As we tucked both of them into bed, Dad gave me a kiss on the head and said, "You're magical."

"Thanks, Dad," I said, feeling proud. My sisters could be a pain sometimes, but I loved them.

"Sophia, I wanted to talk to you about something," Dad said as I headed for my room.

"Okay, but I have some reading to do for English class," I replied, flopping on my bed. "Plus, I'm supposed to have a group chat with my coding group." It was getting late, and I was feeling kind of sleepy.

Dad leaned against my doorframe. He looked tired, too. "The thing is, honey, we're going to need your help with the girls this weekend," he said.

That wasn't a surprise. I turned on the lamp on my nightstand and sighed. Last weekend, my sisters and I had played dress-up and made brownies when my parents went out, and the weekend before that, we'd gone on a scavenger hunt outside. I had fun with them, but I had the hackathon on Saturday. Sunday was my only free day. I blew out my breath. It was going to be a busy weekend.

"What about Mom and Abuela?" I asked, taking my book and tablet out of my backpack. The tablet was a Christmas present—it was one of the cheap ones and could be kind of slow, but I was glad to have it.

Dad looked at me, his eyes sad. "Mom has to work the day shift, and Abuela is going to Marissa's." He paused, weighing his words. "I was asked to give a speech at a real estate conference. I couldn't say no—it could bring me a lot of new clients."

I was going to argue, but was too tired. "Okay, fine," I said resignedly, flipping to the assigned chapter for tonight. "Night, Dad."

That was his cue to leave, but he wasn't moving. He ran his fingers through his hair, which he only did when he was anxious. "Uh, the thing is, sweetie, I need you to watch your sisters on Saturday."

I dropped my book onto my comforter. "What? But Saturday's the hackathon." I'd thought he had been talking about Sunday.

He looked at me apologetically. "I know. I'm sorry, honey. Your mom and I tried to figure something out, but my conference is all day, and we're really in a bind."

I was slowly realizing what was happening, and it did *not* sound good. "Why can't Abuela watch them?"

My dad came over and sat on the bed. "Marissa is going to have surgery on her knee next week. I'm sure everything's going to be fine, but Abuela is worried and wants to accompany her on her last doctor's appointment before the surgery." He ran his fingers through his hair again. "She does so much for our family, Sophia. I—I just didn't want to ask her to cancel her plans with her sister."

A big lump had started to form in my throat. Abuela *did* do so much for our family. I thought about how I would feel if one of my sisters were having surgery. I looked away, trying to hold back the tears, but it didn't help. A tear slid down my cheek, and I angrily swiped it away. "But I had plans! Does that mean *nothing* to you?" As I heard myself, I realized I sounded way ruder than I intended. Dad gave me a stern look, and I cast my eyes down at my book.

"But what am I going to tell my friends, Dad?" I said, glancing up at him. "They're counting on me."

My dad had a sympathetic expression. "I'm so sorry, honey. If there was another way around this, we'd do it." He patted my knee. "I'm sure there will be other hackathons for you to participate in," he said. His phone began to buzz, so he leaned over to kiss the top of my head and walked out.

I rolled onto my stomach, my fists clenched. I couldn't believe my parents were doing this to me. I was so angry, I punched my pillow. Not only was Mom not going to be able to come to the hackathon, now they were saying I couldn't even *go*!

Tyson often said he was tired of getting "the short end of the stick" when he was given a sucky job at football, no matter how hard he worked. I understood what he meant. It didn't matter how much I babysat my sisters or how much I cared about the hackathon—now I wouldn't even be able to participate. I was getting the shortest end of the stick possible.

I flipped over onto my back. I had little glow-in-the-dark stars stuck on my ceiling. When I was younger, I used to make wishes on them. I stared at them now, wishing they could help me.

I knew that we couldn't make any changes to our team after one o'clock tomorrow, or we risked getting disqualified. That meant I should tell my friends now about my problem. But . . . what if I could persuade my dad to get a babysitter, or come up with some other solution? I knew my parents were against having babysitters. The last one had been a disaster. It was a high-school girl named Becky whom Abuela had met at Pearl's dance studio. She'd spent the whole time texting her friends, eaten all of Mom's favorite pretzels, invited her boyfriend over, and ignored my sisters. Lola didn't like her, and it upset my parents. Ever since then, they never felt comfortable with anyone other than family taking care of my sisters. Plus, we didn't exactly have a lot of extra money, and babysitters were expensive. "But maybe I can convince them to do it, just this one time," I muttered to myself.

While I was trying to figure out what to do, Leila's name popped up on the chat screen on my tablet. Mrs. Clark had set up a group chat program for anyone in coding club, which made it easier to have conversations on our computers and share documents for when we talked about coding projects.

Why tell them now? I rationalized. *I could find a babysitter and convince Mom and Dad.* Even though I wasn't *quite* so sure. I knew a few older teenagers—like Tyson; Alex, Lucy's older brother; and I'd just met Tania, Leila's older sister—but I felt weird asking them to babysit. Besides, I knew my parents wouldn't go for anyone they didn't know, after last time.

Erin: soph? u here? everyone else is here!

I didn't answer right away—I was still debating what to do.

Maya: heyyyy have so much homework tonite what is wrong with life 😫 😫 😫
Erin: me too science quiz tomorrow. ugh 😫

Lucy: argh alex keeps telling me how easy middle school is. and he ate all the chips. bros are sooooo annoying 😠 😠 😠 😠

My fingers hovered over the keyboard. I wanted to tell them; I really did. But I couldn't make myself type the words.

Maya: ok, let's start brainstorming. i'm sure s will get here soon

We hadn't gotten much further in our robot plan since last night at my house, and we needed to figure out our robot idea.

Lucy: i have an idea! what if the robot carried blocks in a scoop?

Erin: it could . . . problem is that every block counts as a thing 😣 😣

Maya: hmm . . . maybe the robot could sense the walls in the maze so it'll turn by itself if we code it to. right, leila? 👍 👍

We'd talked about the modules at Maya's after the Bakeshop, and that's what Leila had told us—that some sensors could react to touch.

Leila: yup, that'd work with a button. if the button touches the wall, it'd get activated and the robot would turn right or left, depending on our code

Maya: but wouldn't the robot need a part that a button could attach to for that to work? the rover alone couldn't do that, right?

Leila: oh yeah, that's true . . . 😣 😣 😣

Erin: hmm . . . how about adding a gripper arm? that's one of the modules, right? don't know what it would grip, though . . .

Lucy: or . . . could we use one of the sensors so that the robot could figure out distances and never even have to touch a wall? 😁 😁 😁

Leila: maybe, but might get complicated to code

I decided to forget about my problem and join the chat. I'd gotten myself out of problem situations before; I could handle this one, too. Like Coach often said, "I give you a problem, I want a solution." And solutions were my specialty.

Sophia: could we use the plug-in speakers?

Maya: sophia! you're here! 🙌

Sophia: yeah, sorry, got a little delayed . . . little sisters!

Leila: i can relate! well about a little brother . . . speakers good idea! the robot could play music!

Erin: oooh, he could play dance to the beat!!!

After going back and forth about a bunch of options, we decided that our robot could do everything we'd thought of:

- push a ball
- use a movable arm
- touch sense the walls
- play Erin's song while it moved

Plus, using music totally worked with our Rockin' Robot team name. Erin's song was kind of long, so she sent me the music to edit. We had a program at home to edit sound bites, since my dad needed to edit videos he took of homes for his job. I often edited the audio in videos I took of the football team, so I'd gotten pretty good at it.

Before logging off, we agreed to meet up at lunch the next day to work on our plan for what the robot would do and how we'd make it happen. Yawning, I turned my tablet off and leaned over to plug it in. I'd gotten so caught up in our plans that I'd forgotten I might not be able to even *go* to the hackathon. I'd have to talk to my parents in the morning about getting a babysitter, and if it didn't work, I'd tell my friends the bad news at lunch before 1:00 p.m.

But there was no way I could see myself doing that.

I'd make it work. I always did.

Chapter Five

The next day at school, I had a knot in my stomach all morning. I hadn't been able to corner my mom or dad to talk to them about Saturday—my mom wasn't back from work before I left for school, and my normally hyper-organized dad rushed out so fast, he forgot his travel coffee mug. I texted them with my babysitter idea, but they hadn't responded. They were probably too busy, and I knew they preferred to talk about that kind of stuff in person, anyway.

By the time I got to the cafeteria, my coding group was already at our usual table. I sat down next to Leila and slapped down my lunch bag on the table.

"Those are my favorite kind of granola bars," Leila said as I pulled a chocolate chip pretzel bar from my lunch bag. She held up a matching bar. "Twins!"

"So good," I agreed, unwrapping my bar and taking a big bite.

Erin leaned in. "Get this, I overheard Bradley and his team talking in Spanish class—they have something secret going on—"

"Hang on," I cut Erin off before she could finish. "I need to tell you something." I felt all their eyes on me. "About the hack—"

"Ladies!"

I looked up to see Bradley and his hackathon team—which included Sammy (!)—approaching our table. My stomach clenched like I was on a roller coaster. Bradley was always making jokes, and usually I found him kind of funny. But not today—not right now. I needed to get my bad news off my chest, and being within a foot of Sammy had apparently paralyzed me.

"So, what are your big plans for the hackathon?" Bradley asked in a mocking tone as he and Alicia, Ellie, and Sammy sat down at our table. I hadn't seen Sammy since the awkward wave at the Bakeshop, and I could already feel my face heat up again. It didn't help that he sat down *right* next to me.

"Hey, Soph," he whispered, scooching over on the bench. There wasn't much room for all of us, so I could feel his arm against mine. He had on a navy blue sweatshirt that brushed softly against my wrist. Cue heart thumps.

"Oh, we're still brainstorming," Maya said dismissively. "You were saying, Sophia, before we got so *rudely* interrupted—" She glared at Bradley. I didn't answer, so she kicked my foot under the table. "Soph!"

"Huh? What?"

"You had something you were going to tell us?" Erin prodded.

"Oh, yeah." I didn't want to tell my friends about my hackathon problem in front of everyone. "It's no big deal." I turned to Bradley. "So, um, what's your epic robot idea?"

Mrs. Clark had explained that even though there were prizes—and the chance to get ice cream with her, of course—the hackathon wasn't competitive, and we shouldn't be worried about stealing each other's ideas. It was more about making a cool robot that worked, and helping each other out. In fact, Mrs. Clark told us that there'd be times at the hackathon to share ideas and help other groups with their robots. Still, I was hoping our robot would beat Sammy's team.

"Our idea is so sick," Bradley bragged, pushing back his curly red hair. He rubbed his hands together. "We're going to make a clone army that will take over the school, replace all the teachers, and never assign homework ever again."

Maya rolled her eyes, and the rest of us chuckled. Bradley was known for being ultracompetitive—he was always boasting about how well he did on tests. I wasn't surprised that he didn't want to tell us about their idea.

Leila gave him a sidelong glance. "Wow, a clone army, huh? Sounds like a lot of coding. Are you sure you won't need to clone yourself?"

I laughed. "Burn!" I gave Leila a fist bump.

Bradley gave us a dismissive look. "Totally enough time. We divided the work. Alicia and Sammy are doing the coding." Then he nodded at Ellie. "And she's building the robots." He folded his hands behind his head. "I'm the evil mastermind behind the takeover, obviously."

Ellie punched him lightly in the arm. "Stop being stupid, Bradley," she said seriously, and then looked over at Leila. "Wait, are you all on one team? I thought you were with Mark and Maddie." She reached back to tighten her ponytail.

Erin slung her arm around Leila. "She was, but they had to cancel, so she's in our group now. And she knows *all* about robots."

Bradley raised his eyebrows. "That's cool, but we've got *our* robot *all* figured out."

"Oh yeah? So what's your robot going to do?" Maya asked warily.

"Well, we've got four items picked out," Alicia said, leaning forward. "A movable arm, a sensor to detect walls, a ball, and—"

"Whoa, whoa, whoa, don't tell her!" Bradley cut Alicia off, waving his arms. "You'll ruin the surprise."

I had a bad feeling about the "surprise." Even though the hackathon wasn't competitive, I didn't want our group to build the *exact* same robot as Bradley's team. And so far, it seemed like we'd be using the same modules.

I started thinking that maybe we should go back to the drawing board with our idea. But then I realized that I probably wasn't going to be on the team, so the Rockin' Robots would need to figure that out without me. And they didn't even know it yet. Ugh. This day was going from bad to worse.

I pushed myself away from the table. "I'm going to get some water," I announced, raising my half-full bottle. I just wanted to get away for a minute. Maybe when I got back, Bradley's team would be gone and I could tell my friends about my problem.

"Hold up," Sammy said, drinking his entire water bottle in one long swish. "I'll come with you."

Out of the corner of my eye, I saw my friends exchange looks.

"Remember, bro," Bradley shouted from behind me, "she's the enemy. Don't tell her anything!"

I turned around, scowled at Bradley, and walked away, Sammy falling into step alongside me.

I wasn't usually alone with Sammy—we always hung out in big groups or just texted. I started getting nervous. What were we going to talk about? What if I had bad breath?

"Bradley can be a pain sometimes, but he's cool," Sammy said as we made our way toward the water fountain.

"Yeah, really cool," I said sarcastically, hoping Bradley didn't yell anything else out at us in the crowded cafeteria.

Sammy laughed it off. "So hey, anyway, thanks again for the English homework."

"No problem," I answered a little too excitedly.

We walked in silence for what seemed like forever. Suddenly the water fountain felt like it was a million miles away. I clenched my water bottle so tightly, I thought I might break it.

"So Maya's on the dance committee, right?" Sammy finally asked. His voice cracked a little.

I nodded awkwardly and kept walking. I didn't know

what to say. This was so embarrassing! When we finally reached the water fountain, Sammy held the button while I filled my bottle. Our hands brushed, and I thought my heart was going to jump out of my chest.

"So . . . do you know what the theme is?" he blurted out. I looked up and missed the water stream but pretended to ignore it.

"The theme?" I repeated, confused.

"Yeah, for the dance."

"Oh right, the dance," I said slowly, wondering why he was asking me that. "Um, I don't think it's been decided yet."

"Oh, okay," he answered. We headed back to our table with our filled-up bottles.

I decided I'd had enough of this weird vibe. "So . . . I know I'm the 'enemy,' but what *is* your awesome idea for the hackathon?" I asked. I was determined to say something to make things less awkward . . . and I *was* curious.

Sammy shrugged. "I don't know how awesome it is. It's probably not that different from your group's, anyway."

"Really? Do you think that's okay?"

He nodded. "I don't think it matters if we choose the same modules. The difference will be in how we use them."

"True."

"So . . . what's your secret part?" I pressed forward with my questions, even though the butterflies in my stomach were zooming around like crazy. "You can tell me, Sammy. We've known each other forever, right?" As the words came out of my mouth, I realized how true they were. It was silly to feel weird around him.

He laughed. "Man, Bradley was right . . . you *are* the enemy!" But the way he said it I could tell he didn't really think so. "Seriously, though, Sophia, I can't tell you. You'll just have to wait and find out."

I snorted. "Okay, so on a scale of one to ten, how 'amazing' is the secret part?"

He thought about that for a few seconds. "Fifteen," he finally said.

I laughed. "Fine. Don't tell me. But I can tell you . . . me and my girls aren't worried."

The walk to our table felt a lot shorter than the walk to the water fountain. When we got back, Bradley stood up. "Enough romance, guys—we need to go. We've got work to do!" He raised his arms as if he was the king of the cafeteria and bowed. "And so, we bid you farewell."

Did he say *romance*? I wanted to smack him. Suddenly

the flip-flops in my stomach were back. I couldn't even look at Sammy as he walked away. Instead, I slid into my seat and pretended like nothing had happened.

As soon as they left, Lucy didn't miss a beat. "So . . . spill it, Soph!"

"Romance!" Erin said. "Bradley did say 'romance,' didn't he?"

"Stop. I have ears, you know," I said as I bit into my shiny red apple. "Bradley says a lot of dumb things."

"What's all this about?" Leila asked, gesturing with one hand as she took a sip of her juice.

Maya turned to her. "Sophia has a crush on Sammy, but she refuses to tell us *anything* about it." She gave me an admonishing look.

"Ooh, a crush!" Leila gushed. "I *thought* something might be going on."

"C'mon, Soph, you know you can tell us anything," Erin said, grabbing a handful of her salt and vinegar chips. "And we want to know *everything*."

I kept chomping my apple, but they kept staring at me.

"It was nothing," I finally relented. "He asked me about the dance, and then we talked about our robots." I zipped my sandwich bag closed. "See? Nothing to discuss."

Maya put her hands on the table, her eyes widening.

"Wait, what? You talked about the dance? Did he ask you to go with him?"

"No, of course not!" I scoffed. "He just asked me what the theme was."

They all exchanged glances.

"I *swear* he didn't ask me to the dance! It wasn't even like that!"

Erin folded up her reusable lunch sack. "Well, not this time, but maybe he will soon," she said, sounding like she knew what she was talking about.

"Or, better yet, *you* could ask *him*," Maya added, a devilish grin on her face.

"Totally," Lucy said.

Until then, I hadn't even thought about going to the dance with Sammy. I assumed I'd go to the dance with my friends, like most people did. But then I started to wonder—why *was* Sammy asking me about the theme?

"So, about the hackathon?" Leila said. She must have sensed I didn't want to talk about Sammy anymore. I gave her a grateful look, and she smiled back. "These guys have something up their sleeve, so we need to get to work if we want any chance of winning a prize. We have our idea; now we just need to figure out how to do it." She pulled out a sheet of paper and showed it to us. She'd made columns for the four modules we'd chosen—a ball, an arm, a sensor, and speakers. She'd started to write details in each column.

"Wow, this is really helpful, Leila," Erin said.

Leila smiled bashfully. "Mr. Miller had us watch a movie in history class today, and I'd already seen it, so I figured I'd work on this."

I was feeling more and more guilty about not telling them my problem, so before anything else could interrupt us, I took a deep breath. "Hang on, I need to—"

Maya cut me off. "Lucy, you registered our group, right?" she asked. I'd forgotten that Lucy had volunteered to sign us all up online.

"Yep," she answered, taking her phone out. "I added all of our e-mail addresses, so we should all have confirmations by now."

We grabbed our phones. "Got it!" Maya said, shutting off her phone and putting it back in her pocket. The others nodded and put theirs away, too.

I scanned the information below the confirmation in my e-mail:

"We'd like to remind you that once the official

deadline to register for the hackathon has passed at 1 p.m. on Thursday, there can be no further changes to any team. If all registered participants on the team cannot make it, your team will need to withdraw from the hackathon. You can participate as a team in the next event later this year."

I looked at the clock on the wall, a lump forming in my throat: It was 1:05 p.m. I also remembered that I still hadn't heard from my parents. The Wi-Fi inside school wasn't great, though, and sometimes messages sent from outside the school never made it through. I guess I'd just have to wait until I got home to find out what they thought about getting a babysitter.

The warning bell rang, and everyone started gathering their stuff. My spirits sank. I knew I should just tell them, just blurt it out. But if I told them I had to drop out, I'd be disqualifying my whole team.

My mouth felt dry as I tried to think of the right way to tell them. *Just handle it, Sophia,* I thought. Slowly I crumpled up my lunch bag and picked up my binders.

Erin grabbed her books. "Group chat tonight, girls? We still gotta figure out our algorithm." They all nodded.

"I—I—" I started.

The bell—the real one, not the warning one—rang.

I swallowed hard.

"Hurry up, Soph, we've got to get to class," Lucy said, sounding exasperated.

I raised my phone to show them the time and said in a tight, tearful voice, "It's past one p.m."

They exchanged puzzled glances. "Yeah, so?" Maya said, raising her eyebrows.

I knew there wasn't enough time to explain everything to them. And, anyway, what difference did it make if I told them now or later? We'd still be disqualified. "We better get to class," I said finally.

Maya gave me a weird look but then let it go.

"You okay, Soph?" Lucy prodded as we headed out of the cafeteria.

"Mmm-hmm." I nodded.

"Weirdo," Lucy said, giving me a good-natured shove.

"Takes one to know one!" I said, faking a smile.

As we joined the hordes of people in the hall, the knot in my stomach grew. How was I going to tell them that we'd all have to drop out of the hackathon—all because of *me*?

Chapter Six

"Easy does it," I said to myself, sliding the needle into the black circle with a hole in the middle of it—the valve. Then I turned on the air pump and inflated the football. I'd done this so many times, I could do it in my sleep. Not that Tyson and I enjoyed filling the footballs with air—we had to reset the pump after almost every football was filled, since it was so old and decrepit.

"Yo, don't overinflate it, Soph," he shouted over at me.

I rolled my eyes. He had said that to me after literally every single ball I'd filled this afternoon. Ignoring him, I quickly removed the needle. At least filling footballs took my mind off the hackathon and how I was going to let my team down. I hadn't seen my friends for the rest of the afternoon, so I'd have to tell them tonight during our group chat. Every time I thought about it, my hands got clammy.

I tossed the newly inflated football into the football bin, half listening to Coach's pep talk a few feet away. "A player is nothing without his team," he told the players. "You've gotta watch out for one another. What good is a quarterback if he doesn't have his team backing him up?" They had a game tomorrow, and Coach always gave speeches like that the night before big games.

The guys all put their hands on top of one another's and yelled, "Rise as ONE!"

Football could be so sappy sometimes, but I loved it. No matter what happened in practice, the guys gave it their all at games, and it was true—they always had their teammates' backs. Plus, I loved the structure and order of it all. There were no surprises or changes of rules at the last minute—not like at home.

Tyson was on the bench nearby, cleaning visors and helmets. When he was done, he came over to help me with the footballs. He was tall and skinny, with short hair, and ears that stuck out from his head. He didn't seem like the type to get nervous around people—I had a feeling he had no problems in the romance department, and was pretty sure he'd have advice for me about Sammy. Plus, since he was in high school, he wouldn't even know who I was talking about. It was perfect.

"Hey, Tyson," I said, trying to sound casual. "If you wanted to ask someone to a dance, how would you do it?"

"Um, I'd just ask them," he said, resetting the machine, which had conked out again. "Why?"

"No reason."

He made a face. "You think I'm going to believe that? Come clean, Sophia. Why'd you ask?"

I shrugged, looking down at my sneakers. I didn't like feeling so unsure of myself, but when I was around Sammy, that was exactly how I felt. "It's just, there's this guy, and the winter dance is coming up, and he, um, asked me about the theme, and I was wondering . . ."

"Did he ask you to go with him?"

"No." I was starting to feel stupid for bringing this up.

"Maybe the guy's into you. Or maybe he just wants to be friends."

I thought about that. "He brought up the dance, but he didn't ask me to go to it," I said, feeling more confused.

Tyson looked at me, narrowing his eyes. "Do *you* want to go to the winter dance with him?"

"No," I blurted out. My cheeks were tingling, and by the way Tyson was looking at me, I knew I was blushing. "I mean, I don't know. Maybe!" I looked down at the football machine. "Ugh, I hate this."

But when I glanced up at him, Tyson didn't look fazed at all. He just kept filling up footballs and chucking them into the bin. "Just be yourself, Sophia," he told me. "You're a cool girl. If this dude doesn't want to go to the dance with you, his loss."

I waited for a second, not sure if he was joking. "Well, thanks," I said. Tyson threw a ball at me, and I caught it.

"Nice catch," he said, grinning.

"Yeah, I usually am able to catch those three-foot passes," I said sarcastically.

"Now there's the Sophia I know!" Tyson said, laughing.

I tried to smile back. Now that I thought about it, whether or not Sammy wanted to ask me to the dance, I knew that he was my friend. And once I told my coding team I was dropping out of the hackathon, I was going to need all the friends I had.

When I got home from school, my parents weren't home yet. For dinner, Abuela made her famous tortilla soup with extra chopped green onion, just like I like it, but I couldn't even enjoy it. Later that night, I logged on to my computer and opened the chat program. I'd tell my friends fast, like ripping off a Band-Aid. Lucy would be

mad. I knew how excited she was about the hackathon—
she'd wanted to do it before Mrs. Clark even told us about
it in coding club. I hadn't been friends with Maya and Erin
for that long, but they'd probably be mad, too, especially
since we'd already put so much work into our robot idea.
And Leila had been so happy when we asked her to be
part of our group. *Sigh.*

Suddenly my screen lit up.

Maya: hey!!!

So far, Maya was the only one on.

Sophia: hey

I wanted to tell them all at once, so I waited for the
others.

Lucy and Leila finally logged in. Now we were just
waiting for Erin.

Lucy: so, i have an idea for the algorithm

I knew that once we started talking about our robot
plans, it'd be hard to change the topic.

Sophia: can we wait for erin? i have something to
tell u guys

Lucy: what? is this what you were acting so weird about today????

Sophia: i

I'd only typed one letter when the ding on the chat announced that Erin had arrived.

Sophia: we have a problem

Erin: is this about whatever happened at lunch?

Sophia: kind of. i

Knock knock

"Sweetie?" I heard my mom say outside my door.

I stopped typing and looked away from the computer for a second. "Come in!" It wasn't good timing, but I knew Mom would be mad at me if I didn't let her in.

Sophia: hold on, moms here

My mom came over and kissed my cheek. "Hi, honey. I got your text. So we have a little problem, huh?"

"What's your definition of 'little'?" I said, crossing my arms across my chest. My mom was looking around my room at the mess of papers and clothes. Normally I kept my room superclean, but I'd been too distracted this week.

"Can I … sit down?" Mom asked, waving vaguely toward my bed.

I nodded and got up to clear a spot.

"Sometimes, honey," Mom said, sitting back on the bed and crossing her legs, "we all have to make hard decisions."

"I know." I glanced over at my computer quickly.

Lucy: sophia? you back yet?

Mom gave me a sympathetic look. "I know you were looking forward to the hackathon, honey, but Dad and I really need you here on Saturday."

"Yeah, I *know.*" I didn't want to be a brat about it, but it was starting to feel like I didn't matter at all. "But I *told* you about the hackathon." It was a done deal now, so it wouldn't make a difference, but I couldn't help telling my mom how I felt. "I know you're busy, and I get that Dad has a work thing, but couldn't you get how important this is to me?" I said. "Why do *I* always have to fill in for everyone?" I added. Against my will, my eyes were filling with tears. I hated crying—especially in front of people.

My mom looked shocked. "Honey. That's not how it is at all. We—"

"No, that's *exactly* how it is!" I cried without thinking. "I'm working really hard at school, and football, and coding club, but none of that even matters, because the minute you have something to do, it means I have to stop *everything* to help you. I'm so sick of it!" Now I was really crying.

My mom sat quietly for a moment. She looked a little shocked at my outburst. "Do you want a tissue?" she asked finally. I nodded, and she went over to the tissue box on my dresser to get me one.

"I think I need the whole box," I said, blowing loudly.

She managed to give me a small smile, but her eyes were creased with concern. "Sweetie, I'm really sorry about all this. I know you have a lot of responsibility around here as the oldest sibling, and Dad and I really, truly appreciate how much you help out at home." She took a deep breath. "If—if we made you feel like your plans didn't matter, I'm sorry. That's not how we think or how we feel. I guess sometimes grown-ups get caught up in things and might not see things from their kids' point of view."

"You can say *that* again," I muttered.

My mom reached out and wrapped her arms around me tightly. "I didn't realize you were so upset about this. I wish I could change things, but we're really in a bind."

"I know, it's just...," I choked out. "I *really* wanted to go to the hackathon. Coding club is, like, the only place where I have my own...my own group," I said, realizing how much

I cared about my "permanent group." "And everyone from the club's going to be there . . ." I stopped short of telling her about Sammy. "And I haven't even been able to tell my friends yet, and now they're going to be disqualified, all because of *ME*!" More tears slid down my face.

"Disqualified?" Mom echoed. She looked confused.

"Yeah, those are the rules if someone cancels." I took a gulp of air. "And we passed the deadline to make changes."

"Oh, honey," my mom said, rubbing my back. "I wish I could help fix this. But why didn't you tell your friends sooner?"

"I *tried*!" I cried. The truth was, I hadn't wanted to tell them because I thought I could handle it on my own. And clearly I was wrong.

My computer kept dinging. My friends were probably wondering where I was.

My mom looked at me. "Sweetie, I do feel bad about all this. I think your friends will understand, though. They know you have responsibilities at home, too—we all do."

"Maybe," I said, sniffling. "But it affects them, too." Thinking about my friends made me feel guilty all over again about letting them down. I decided I had to give it one more try. I looked up at my mom pleadingly. "Can't we get a babysitter, just this one time?" I knew finding one would be a challenge, but I couldn't help bringing it up.

"You know how Dad and I feel about babysitters after Becky," she said, wrinkling her nose like she was smelling something rotten. Then she looked down at her knees. "Especially with Lola not handling new situations so well." She gave me a look. "Plus, we're not in a position to spend the extra money right now—you know that, Sophia."

I could feel tears welling up again. I tried to hold them back, but they started slipping down my cheeks.

"Oh, honey," my mom said. "Don't cry."

"I'm not crying!" I burst out as I sobbed.

I could tell Mom was thinking things through. "Although . . . there's a family that moved into that white house with the blue shutters on Lucy's street that has a teenage daughter. I've met her and her mom a couple times when I was walking with Rosie. The daughter's name is Monica. She seemed really nice."

Monica. My mom had just thrown me a life preserver, and I grabbed it with all my might. "Let's ask Dad if we can have Monica babysit!" I said excitedly. I felt a glimmer of hope that Mom was even considering this.

Mom stood up. "Let me talk to him and see if we can work something out."

I put my hands on my heart. "Really?"

"I'm not making any promises." Mom pointed at my computer screen. "And you should tell your friends what's going on. It's always best to be honest, Sophia. You should give your friends a little more credit. They might just surprise you."

Down the hall, Pearl shouted, "Mooooooooommmmm!"

"Coming!" My mom sighed as she walked out.

After my mom left, I got back on my computer.

Sophia: hey i'm back
Erin: finally! so what's the problem?

Mom was right, I should be honest with my friends. But what was the point of worrying them if we could get Monica to babysit?

Sophia: we need to do our pseudocode
Lucy: umm . . . duh
Maya: that was the big problem???
Sophia: yeah
Sophia: ok i started a shared doc

We chatted about how to make our robot and ended up with this:

The Rockin' Robots Pseudocode
We start with a rover base with four wheels and an

attached motherboard. The motherboard has four slots for plug-in modules. Our first plug-in is a large arm that swings freely. Our second module is plug-in speakers, which will start playing automatically.

Next will be a button. We will write code so that if the robot hits a wall and activates the button, the robot will turn left and left again, until it is not facing the wall and can continue through the maze.

The last part is a ball. The arm will push it along like it's playing soccer. The robot will move through the maze entirely on its own with our program.

Sophia: done. this is awesome.
Leila: epic!

I was proud of our robot plan. It was amazing to think of how much we'd learned since our first coding club meeting! As we all logged off, I thought, *Now all I have to do is make sure Dad and Mom agree that:*

a. we can get a babysitter

b. Monica is able to babysit, and

c. my friends don't get disqualified and hate me forever.

Otherwise the only *epic* thing was going to be my *epic* fail.

Chapter Seven

On Fridays, sixth-graders had study hall in the morning, so Lucy, Leila, and I were planning to work on the algorithm part of our robot plan.

The study hall room had big tables with chairs instead of the individual desks we had in our regular classrooms. Lucy was already sitting at one of them when I arrived.

"Hey, Lu," I said, pulling up a chair next to her.

"Hey, Soph," she said. She had green studs that matched her green zip-up hoodie. "TGIF!"

"Totally," I said, heaving a sigh. It had been a long week.

We'd just started looking through the hackathon binder when Leila arrived. She seemed kind of out of breath.

"Sorry I'm late, guys," she huffed, pulling up a chair.

I moved my books to make room for her. "Everything okay?" I asked.

Leila sighed. "Ugh, my little brother," she said, shaking crumbs off her sleeve. "My parents asked me to help get him ready for school this morning, and he decided his new favorite art supply was toothpaste."

I winced. "Yeesh."

Lucy turned to me. "Didn't Pearl do that once?"

I snorted. "If you're referring to the Great Peanut Butter Incident, then yes." That was so long ago, I could almost laugh at it. Almost.

"Just let me know if I have any in my eyebrows still," Leila said, gesturing to her forehead. "My whole face feels minty fresh."

"No, you're good," I said, inspecting her. "Trust me, I *know* how annoying little kids can be. After the hackathon, I swear we should build a sibling-taming robot."

"The Babysitter 3000!" Leila suggested.

"We just have to find a material that's toothpaste and peanut butter proof," Lucy added, and we all chuckled.

"Speaking of which, how is our robot coming along?" Leila asked.

"Lucy and I were just looking at the different modules," I said. "The robot needs to move forward and turn when it senses the walls, right?"

"Right." Leila jotted something down and showed it

to us. "If it hits a wall and activates the button we'll put on the front of it, we can code it so that it'll turn again and again until it's not touching the wall and can move through the maze."

"Like this?" Lucy stood up to imitate the robot. A few people gave her strange looks, but she didn't care.

Across the room, I heard Bradley and Sammy laughing. We'd been so focused on our robot plan that I hadn't even noticed Sammy until now. But after what Tyson had told me at football practice, I didn't feel quite as nervous around him. Besides, Sammy probably just liked me as a friend.

Sammy had gotten up and was hitting the wall, just like Lucy. I realized they must be prepping for the hackathon, too. It looked like they didn't just have the same idea as us—they were going to code it similarly, too. I wondered what their big surprise was going to be.

But by the end of study hall, Leila, Lucy, and I got so engrossed in our modules that I didn't even notice what Sammy and his team were doing.

The football team's game was away, and Tyson and I had the night off. When I got home after school, I opened the front door, expecting to see Abuela and my sisters in the kitchen. But no one was there.

I hung up my jacket. "Hello?" I called out.

"Upstairs!" Dad's voice rang out.

"Dad! You're home early," I said, running upstairs to his bedroom. I gave him a hug. "Where is everyone?" He was throwing clothes into a small black suitcase, a semi-panicked look on his normally calm face.

"Mom and Abuela are with the girls. Mom said she'd bring home pizza when they got back."

"Sounds good—I'm starving." I plopped down on the bed. "What are you doing?" His dresser drawers were open, and there were clothes hanging from them.

"There's been a change of plans. I need to go to the conference tonight. I was asked to attend the opening banquet, so I'm leaving in . . ." He glanced at the clock by the bed. "Ten minutes."

"And you're not freaking out?" I asked, only half-kidding. My dad was the type to schedule dental appointments a year in advance.

"Not yet," he said, yanking some shirts off hangers, sending the hangers clattering to the floor. He shot me a glance. "Okay, maybe just a slight freak-out."

"Here," I said, grabbing the shirts and folding them into neat piles. "Let me help."

"Thanks, honey." He threw ties onto the bed and looked

around haphazardly. "With all of us gone tomorrow, I'm going to need you to take care of some chores."

I stopped folding. Chores? Tomorrow?

"Wait, Dad—Mom talked to you about Monica, right?" I'd assumed it was taken care of, but now I was getting worried.

"Monica? No," he said, tossing two more ties onto the bed. "Which one do you like better?"

I pointed to the one with red and gray stripes, but I had a sinking feeling in my stomach. "Mom said she was going to talk to you last night. Did you guys not talk?"

He stuffed some socks into his suitcase. "No, I got home late." He looked around the room. "Grab my shoes, will you?" He pointed to his black loafers near his dresser.

I picked them up and tossed them like footballs one by one to my dad. He caught them easily. "Mom said she'd talk to you about having Monica babysit tomorrow so I could go to the hackathon."

"Well, she didn't mention it to me," he said, putting his shoes in a pocket of the suitcase. He started going through papers on his dresser. "Listen, honey, I'm sorry, but there's nothing I can do about it now. We're all going to be away, and I told you I need you to look after your sisters."

I couldn't believe this was happening. "But, Dad, Mom said she would tell you—if I back out now, my *whole* team will get disqualified." I could feel the blood starting to whoosh into my ears. I walked up to his dresser to get his attention. "And we already have a name and everything—the Rockin' Robots. We even made our T-shirts!"

He stopped what he was doing to look at me. "Well, honey, I don't know what to say. You should have told your friends sooner that you couldn't go. You've known for a few days already."

My heart started thumping—but not for the same reasons it recently had. I couldn't bear the thought of letting my team down. "But Mom and I talked! She was going to ask Monica!" I didn't like to sound like I was whining, but this was definitely a getting-the-short-end-of-the-stick moment.

"Who's Monica?" my dad said, only half listening to me. "Where's my belt?" he mumbled, rummaging through his closet.

"Monica's Lucy's new neighbor. Mom was going to see if she could babysit." I saw his belt draped over a chair and handed it to him. *Stay calm,* I told myself, taking a deep, steadying breath. Screaming at people usually didn't make them do what you wanted them to do.

"Thanks, hon." He set the belt and a jacket in his suitcase and turned to me. "Soph, I know how much you want to go to the hackathon, and I do feel bad about this.

But I don't know who Monica is, I'm about to leave on a trip, and I just can't deal with all this right now—it's too last-minute." He looked around the room again. "Can you grab me some paper? There should be paper, over there on the nightstand. I need to give you a list of the chores that need to get done tomorrow. I was going to do a lot of this myself, and now I won't have time."

I'd heard his tone before, and I knew it was going to be impossible to change his mind. Unless . . .

"Dad, if I get the chores done by tomorrow before the hackathon, Monica can babysit, *and* I pay her with my allowance, can I go?"

Dad sighed and ran his hand though his hair. I could tell I was wearing him down. "Okay," he finally said. "I'll talk to Mom about this Monica. But you don't have to pay for a babysitter, honey. We can do that."

I clapped my hands and squealed. He pointed at me. "And I'll *consider* it *only* if the chores are done."

I couldn't find paper on his nightstand, so I took out my phone. "I'll film you." I held up the phone and pressed record. "Tell me what you want me to get done before I go to the hackathon."

"Okay—run the dishwasher, fold the laundry that's in the dryer, and put in the new load that's next to the machine.

And put it all away when it's done."

"Got it." I nodded, still filming. "Anything else?"

"Vacuum the living room, help the girls put away their toys, and *please* convince Pearl to let you wash her leotard..."

I was beginning to get worried that my plan wasn't such a good plan, after all. This was sounding like a lot of chores, even for someone as organized as me.

My dad was still rattling off tasks. "Water the plants, help Lola feed her fish..." When my dad paused, my finger hovered over the stop button. I hoped he was done.

"You're excellent at managing things," he said. "So have your sisters help you. Maybe you can make it into one of those games you play with them." He gave me a sly smile. "Though maybe let them win once in a while."

I stopped the recording and set down my phone. I could handle pretty much anything, but this was a super long list. There was no way I could do all that before the hackathon, even if I started tonight. And although I'd worn my dad down about Monica, I knew he wouldn't relent on this. A deal was a deal, and he wasn't one to bend the rules.

Then it hit me: I was going to have to tell my friends the hackathon was off.

Chapter Eight

That night, I texted the Rockin' Robots. I'd wasted enough time. Time to rip off the Band-Aid.

> **I can't go tomorrow** (ST)

I waited a second before sending another text.

> **my parents need me to take care of my sisters. i tried to get out of it, but no dice** (ST)

Maya responded right away.

> what??? . . . like you cant go to the hackathon?? (MC)

> **yeah . . .** (ST)

> **ER** but wait . . . doesn't this mean we all get disqualified?? >:< >:<

This is what I'd been dreading.

> **ST** yeah, looks like it . . . 😕

No one responded for a few seconds.

> **ST** i'm so so so srry. i tried to get someone to babysit but I couldnt . . . my dad also wants me to do a ton of chores . . . and they have to get done before the hackathon. 😠 😠

Silence.

> **ST** i feel terrible. i'm so sorry. i let you guys down . . . 😕

All I wanted to do was turn off my phone and climb into bed, pull the covers over my head, and not come out for the next few days.

> **LD** soph, are u sure u can't go?

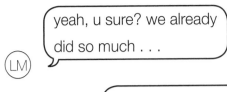
(LM) yeah, u sure? we already did so much . . .

i know . . . so sorry guys . . . i feel awful. . . . (ST)

I decided to be completely truthful. I'd kept the information from them long enough.

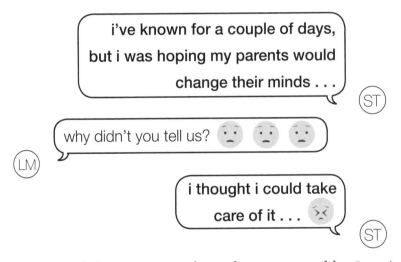
i've known for a couple of days, but i was hoping my parents would change their minds . . . (ST)

why didn't you tell us? (LM)

i thought i could take care of it . . . (ST)

I watched the screen as three dots appeared by Lucy's name and then disappeared. What could she say? I stared at my screen. What could *I* even say?

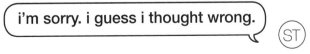
i'm sorry. i guess i thought wrong. (ST)

93

I put my phone down, but the second I did, it started dinging like crazy.

it's ok, soph 🖤
LD

you tried
ER

you have a lot going on right now
MC

I couldn't believe they were being so nice—it almost made me feel worse. I wasn't sure I would have reacted that way if it'd been one of them.

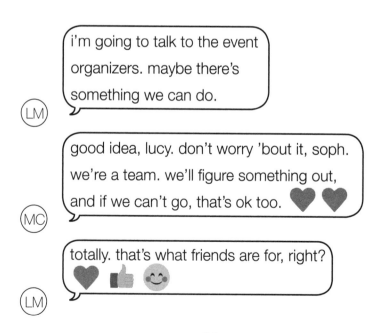

i'm going to talk to the event organizers. maybe there's something we can do.
LM

good idea, lucy. don't worry 'bout it, soph. we're a team. we'll figure something out, and if we can't go, that's ok too. 🖤 🖤
MC

totally. that's what friends are for, right? 🖤 👍 😊
LM

I clutched my phone, feeling my heart warm. Maybe my mom was right. Why hadn't I just told them earlier?

> thanks so much guys. you're the best. and just in case, i'll send you all the edit i made of dance to the beat so you have it for tomorrow. i hope they let you go! break a robot leg! (ST)

I crawled into my bed and pulled the covers over my head. I'd nearly fallen asleep when I realized I hadn't done the one thing I'd promised. Leaning up on one elbow, I grabbed the phone from my nightstand and sent off the edited song.

As I drifted off to sleep, I hoped it'd work out and that my team could still participate in the hackathon without me. If not, I was sure I was going to feel guilty *forever.*

The next morning, I was awake before the sun had barely risen. Abuela had gotten me up when she left for Marissa's. Mom was at work, and Dad was already at his conference.

It wasn't even seven when Rosie came toddling into my room, asking for breakfast.

"Too early," I mumbled, putting my pillow over my head.

"No peekaboo," Rosie argued, pounding the pillow with her little fist. "Bweakfast!"

"Good thing I like you," I grumped, putting on my fuzzy slippers and stomping downstairs after her. Thankfully Rosie had to take the stairs slowly, which suited my tired self perfectly. Pearl and Lola were awake, too, but they weren't hungry yet. They were building a tower with blocks in the living room—I was just glad they were occupied, for the time being.

I still felt sluggish, but I'd mustered enough energy to pour Rosie a bowl of dry cereal when the doorbell rang.

Ring ring

Ring ring ring

Ring ring ring ring

"Bell!" Rosie shouted, and threw cereal at me. "Wucy! Wucy!"

I stared at my little sister. She was pretty observant for a two-year-old, because there *was* only one person we knew who was impatient enough to ring the bell that many times.

But why would Lucy be here now? "No more throwing cereal," I warned, and ran to answer the door.

"Good morning!" Lucy trilled. She was wearing her Rockin' Robots shirt and had a broom in her hand.

"Huh?" I blinked, willing my eyes to wake up faster. "Lu, what are you doing here? It's not even eight a.m. And it's a Saturday."

"Funny you ask!" Lucy exclaimed, stepping aside as Erin, Maya, and Leila joined her on the porch. They must have been hiding behind the bushes. Lucy walked right past me into the kitchen.

Leila grinned. "Hey, Sophia!" She was carrying a sponge and a little bag that said "Fish Food" on the side.

Maya had a watering can and followed Lucy into the kitchen. "Hi, Rosie." She popped some of Rosie's cereal in her mouth. "Yum, my fave."

Erin was the last one to come into the house. She had a huge tote bag slung over her shoulder. I moved aside to let her in but reached out to grab her arm as she passed by. "What's going on?"

She smiled at me. "We had a chat without you."

I swallowed. That didn't sound good. Did they talk about what a terrible person I was to bail out at the last minute?

Erin read my expression. "You goof! Don't worry, it wasn't anything bad. We talked about what to do. We could have tried to go to the hackathon without you—or we could find a way to go *with* you."

"What do you mean, with me?" I repeated, confused. "I *told* you guys I can't go."

Erin winked. "That's what *you* think." She breezed past me and into the kitchen.

My head still felt a bit foggy, but what Erin said made no sense. I followed her to where my friends were sitting and chatting with Rosie, who was loving the attention. I went to sit at the counter, but Maya held out her arm to stop me. "Nope, there's no time for sitting if we're going to get all those chores done!"

Now I was starting to get annoyed. "What are you talking about?" I looked around at all of them. "You guys have *got* to tell me what's going on. It's too early for this."

"We only have three hours." Lucy pointed to the oven clock. "If we want to get to the hackathon on time, we'd better get started!"

"But I *told* you I can't go," I exclaimed, pouring myself a glass of orange juice. "I don't know what you have planned, but my dad . . ."

Lucy interrupted me. "Didn't he say if the chores were done, you could go?"

"Well, sort of . . . ," I clarified. "He said he'd *consider* it."

"So let's get moving!" Erin said cheerfully. She pulled a container of laundry detergent pods out of her tote bag. "We brought everything we need. We couldn't take the chance that there was no fish food or laundry detergent."

I was so confused. "But how do you even know what chores I have to do?"

Maya smiled at me. "You sent us the wrong file, silly."

"What? No, I—" I crossed the kitchen and picked up my phone from the counter. "Oh." In my tired, sad stupor last night, I'd accidentally sent them the video of Dad's list of chores instead of Erin's song!

My mind caught up with what was happening.

"Okay, I get what you're trying to do, and I really appreciate it, but it won't work," I announced, holding up my palms. We'd have to get *all* the chores done in just a few hours before the hackathon, and, anyway, who would watch my sisters if I was out all afternoon?

"Monica will be here at ten," Leila said, as if she were reading my thoughts. "We confirmed this morning."

My mouth fell open. "What? But how . . ."

"Lucy said she was her neighbor. She's babysat my little brother before, so I had her number," Leila explained.

"Oh," I said again, my eyes traveling over my friends' eager faces. "Look, I really appreciate all of this, but trust me, it's not so easy to convince my dad when he has his mind set on something, especially when he's on a work trip . . ."

"We'll text him when we're done," Lucy said simply, sounding like the problem solver she was. "We can send him a video of how clean and neat everything is." She glanced over at Rosie's messy face and added, "Including your sisters."

"Let's be sure to send him the right video," Erin added with a laugh. She handed Lucy a wet paper towel to wipe off Rosie.

Rosie giggled as Lucy played peekaboo with the towel. For once, I stood speechless.

"Okay, Rockin' Robots, we've got work to do!" Maya set the alarm on her phone for a half hour before the hackathon and held up her broom. "Ready, set, go!"

Three hours later, the house sparkled. My sisters were all fed and happy. Even Pearl's ballet costume had been washed. (Maya had convinced her to play dress-up while I did the laundry, making sure to keep the laundry pods away from curious little hands.) It was amazing how much you could get done when you had four friends— your team—helping you. Coach was right: A player was nothing without her team.

Erin and Lucy had watered the plants and taken the newspapers out, and I had vacuumed. Leila had fed Lola's fish with her and even set up a machine to feed them later. The coolest thing was that it used Lola's toys. Lola would knock over a domino that hit a piece of wood, which knocked a ball. The ball opened a chute on a slide, and a little bit of food went down the slide into the fish tank. Leila explained it was called a Rube Goldberg machine—a machine that uses a chain reaction to do something simple. Lola thought it was the best thing ever. Leila promised to come back later to make a different Rube Goldberg machine to help Lola "feed" her dolls.

"How did you all even think of this?" I asked them as we gathered up all the cleaning supplies.

Erin smiled. "It was Leila's idea," she told me.

"That's what friends are for, right?" Leila said bashfully. I gave her a tight hug. It was hard to believe that Leila had only been in our group for a few days. It already felt like she had been part of our "permanent group" forever.

We took a video of the house and my sisters (who of course put on a dance performance). I sent it to my dad and told him that Monica was ready to come over. My friends were crowded around me, waiting for my dad's reply.

Pretty soon three little dots popped up on my screen.

"He's writing!" Erin squealed. Lucy squeezed my hand in solidarity.

> Impressive job, Rockin' Robots. Great teamwork. Code away!

(D)

"Yes!" Lucy shouted as my friends high-fived one another and grinned at me.

"Wow," I said, struggling to find the right words to say. Looking at my friends' faces, a wave of guilt washed over me. I'd been so busy thinking about myself—and so determined to do things alone—that I had almost ruined everything.

"Sometimes it's okay to ask for help, you know," Lucy said softly, reading my mind. "Now go get your T-shirt, Soph. We've got a hackathon to go to!"

Chapter Nine

"It looks like a carnival in here!" Lucy exclaimed as we entered the community center gym.

I took Lucy's hand and gave it a squeeze. It felt like ages since our first coding club meeting. We were ready to rock: Lucy was wearing her sparkly red heart studs, and I had on my lucky star hoodie.

We walked under a massive balloon arch. Multicolored pennants hung from the ceiling, and there was a table with free snacks and drinks. Signs marked the bathrooms, and loud music was playing. Not that we needed it: I could *feel* the excitement in the air. I'd been to the community center tons of times for basketball games before, but I'd never seen so many people packed inside. It felt like another world.

A large sign on the wall announced the schedule:

I leaned toward Lucy. "I wonder what the special activity is."

"Me too!" she squealed. "This is so awesome!"

There were streamers across the ceiling and posters on the walls advertising companies that were sponsoring the event—there was even one for the Bakeshop with images of cake pops all over it, and my mouth started watering.

"Look!" Maya pointed at one poster.

Erin eyed the poster. "OMG, this sounds amazing."

"It really does," Leila said, looking around the rest of the gym.

We made our way through winding aisles of tables full of laptops. There were kids hanging around in clusters, but I didn't see anyone I recognized. I wondered if Sammy and his group were here yet.

"C'mon, guys," Maya said, leading us to the registration table. She told the woman behind the table our team name, and we got name tags and tote bags. I peeked inside and saw granola bars, water bottles, an apple, and a book about coding.

We were assigned to a table in the center of the gym. As we nudged past groups of kids on our way toward our area, someone tapped me on the shoulder. It was Fatima—a girl I knew from basketball camp. "Wow, hi!" I said, giving her a quick hug. "I didn't know you coded!"

She grinned. "I was going to say the same thing to you!" We talked for a minute, and then I rushed to catch up to my friends.

"Hey! Sophia!"

I turned and saw Marco, who went to another middle school. He managed his school's basketball team.

He told me his team was called Coding Whizzes, and that their robot was going to blink and talk. "What's your robot gonna do, Soph?" Marco asked me.

"We're using a movable arm for one of the modules and—"

"Sophia!" I heard from across the room. It was Daisy and Rachel McIntyre. They waved at me. Their parents owned a popular sports store in our town.

Maya looked over at me. "Jeez, do you know *everyone* here?"

Before I could finish telling Marco what our robot was going to do, the start of the hackathon was announced. Teams moved quickly to their tables. I hurried to join mine. Each of us had our own laptop, and there were pencils and scrap paper for us to share.

"To begin the day, we'll be doing an icebreaker," a voice called over the loudspeaker. "Near your computers you'll find a sheet of yellow paper."

I picked up the paper. "It has a bunch of questions on it," I whispered to the others.

The announcer continued, "Your task is to find students, teachers, or volunteers at today's event who can answer the questions. Then, get that person's signature. The winning team will be the first to get signatures for all twenty questions. And there's a prize for the winners."

When the announcer said, "Go!" I read the first question out loud. "Find someone who has moved to town from another state. It can't be someone in your group."

For the next fifteen minutes, we went around the room meeting students from other schools and finding out who loved movies, who read mysteries, and who had dogs. It was a bit awkward at first, but since everyone was doing the same thing, we didn't feel awkward for too long—plus, I knew a lot of kids there, so it made it easier to find people to answer the questions. Within about ten minutes, we had most of the questions answered. But there was one blank we were having trouble filling.

It said: *Find someone who worked on MARS.*

"That's such a weird question," I said, tapping my pencil on my chin. "No one has ever *been* to Mars."

"There are some people I'd like to send there," Erin said with a smirk.

"For real," Lucy said, bobbing her head.

"Can I see the paper?" Leila asked me. I handed it over. "It's M-A-R-S, not Mars. All in capital letters."

"M-A-R-S," Maya repeated. "What could the letters stand for?"

"Oh!" Lucy said, snapping her fingers. "I know! Mobile Autonomous Robotic Systems! I read about it in my mom's TechTown newsletter. It's a new robot Ana Kamat is making."

We rushed across the gym to where Ms. Kamat was unloading boxes from a cart. She had long black hair clasped loosely in a big clip and was wearing a burgundy-colored blazer.

"Hi, Ms. Kamat," Lucy said breathlessly. "We're the Rockin' Robots. We were just wondering—have you worked on MARS?"

Ms. Kamat looked up at us. "Why yes, I have!" she said warmly. We gave her our paper, and she signed her name in the blank. "Which Rockin' Robot figured it out?"

We all looked at one another. "We worked together," I said, gesturing toward all of us.

"Lovely," Ms. Kamat said. "It's so nice to meet you all. Since you figured it out first, you get a prize." She handed us TechTown string backpacks. I glanced inside and saw sunglasses and a box labeled "Fitness Tracker." I'd heard of those—my mom had some that she recommended to patients who were trying to be more active. They helped keep track of how much you exercised.

"Thanks!" we all said at pretty much the same time. I hadn't realized we'd be getting such cool freebies—it made me want to win even more!

Ms. Kamat smiled at us. "I have a good feeling about the Rockin' Robots," she whispered. "Good luck today."

After the icebreaker ended, it was time to start working on our robots. One of the judges walked around the room handing out robot rovers and motherboards and told us that we could pick up our modules from a table in the middle of the gym. Maya and I headed toward the table while Erin, Leila, and Lucy stayed behind to connect our laptops to the motherboard.

A woman at the table handed us a form to list our four modules. "The judges need to see exactly what each team took," she explained.

Mrs. Clark was at the table, too, which was crowded with students picking their modules. "If you change your mind at any time," she told us over the noise, "you can come back and make a trade." With her long layered dark hair, stylish gray glasses, and chunky black boots, Mrs. Clark looked like someone's older sister—not a middle school teacher.

"I think we're set," I said. "A ball, arm, button, and speakers, please."

She handed us our modules. "Good for you for being prepared."

Behind me, I heard a familiar voice say, "We'll take what they're taking . . ."

Then I heard a low, throaty chuckle.

Maya and I spun around, and Bradley and Sammy grinned at us. As soon as I saw Sammy, my heart started racing. Ugh, why was this happening? I'd been fine in study hall the other day. But he was looking awfully cute in his green sweater . . .

Maya looked Bradley up and down. He was wearing his team shirt that said MACHINE MADNESS in a blocky font. No one else was wearing their team T-shirts yet—I didn't think we were supposed to until the end. "How's world domination going?" she asked him, cocking an eyebrow.

Bradley held up a mechanical arm. "We're one step closer to my goal."

Mrs. Clark held out the button, a ball, and the speakers. "Here are the other modules the girls took, if you want the same ones."

"Yeah, thanks, Mrs. C." Bradley turned to us with a smirk. "Our plans changed."

I was still tongue-tied, but it wasn't like Sammy was saying anything, either. I couldn't tell if he was looking at me or at the modules I was holding.

"Wow, you're copying us. What a surprise," Maya said, frowning hard. "No more robot clone army?"

"Oh, there will still be an army, Maya Banana, but not today. First, we must conquer the maze." Bradley pointed to where the maze was set up in the back of the gym. "C'mon, dude, let's go." He gestured to Sammy.

Sammy started to walk away. Then he turned back to me. "See you at the finish line, Sophia."

I nodded meekly. What was *wrong* with me?

"Okay, he's definitely going to pay for using my name and a fruit in the same sentence," Maya scoffed as we headed back to our table. She adjusted the mechanical arm and sensor. "Sammy was totally staring at you, by the way."

I gave her a sideways look and moved my modules to one arm. "No he wasn't."

"Um, Soph, I have eyes, you know. How did you not notice?"

"Because he wasn't."

"If he wasn't, then I'm Maya Banana," she countered, pushing her way through the crowded room.

We passed the maze on our way back to our table and took a peek at it. It looked like the size of one of the football bins in the equipment shed—about six feet long on each side. It wasn't very high, but there were a lot of walls for robots to get around. The outer wall came about to my knee, and was made of high blocks. The inner walls were stiff cardboard and weren't as high—they only reached my ankle. The maze was painted red and had inspirational lines on the walls like *Way to go!* and *You're almost there!*

Maya and I turned to each other, clutching the modules in our hands.

The intensity of the moment hit us. "Let's do this, Soph," Maya said, a determined look on her face.

I nodded. "Time for the Rockin' Robots to rise . . . as one!"

Chapter Ten

The next few hours flew by. Leila named our robot Zahira, which she said meant "shining light" in Arabic, and we all agreed it was perfect.

We set up our modules on Zahira's motherboard and started entering the code we'd discussed into our computers. Everything seemed to be going seamlessly, but when we gave Zahira a test run on our table . . . she wouldn't move.

We tried to change the code a few times, but nothing was working.

"Um, guys? I think we need help," Erin said, pointing to the wall behind our table that said HELP ME. The judges had explained that students could post coding issues there with sticky notes so that teams could help one another out.

"I wish we could figure it out on our own," Leila said, biting her lip. She was still tinkering with code on her computer. "Wait, I have an idea!" She leaned over my shoulder. "Try changing the number in the code from one to five. See what happens then."

"Okay." I made the change. But Zahira still wouldn't move.

Mrs. Clark always said that a big part of coding was problem-solving when things didn't work—fixing bugs. But the harder I stared at the issue, the more the coding started swimming in front of my eyes. And that was when I saw it.

"Guys, wait a minute." I tapped the screen. "Look at this code."

It read:

```
moveForward( )
```

"Anything missing?" I prompted, wanting my friends to see what I was seeing.

Maya nibbled on her lip. "Um . . ."

Leila stared intently at the computer. "I'm not seeing it, Sophia."

"We're missing a semicolon after we call the function!" I exclaimed.

It needed to be:

```
moveForward( );
```

Erin smacked her forehead with her palm. "You're right, Sophia!" We'd learned in coding club that sometimes a semicolon let a computer know that it was the end of a line of code—without it, the computer wouldn't know what instruction to follow. I couldn't believe that a measly semicolon had almost ruined our project. I inserted the semicolon into the code, and miraculously, Zahira began to move.

"Wahoo!" Maya whooped. We all high-fived one another.

"That's what I'm talking about," Lucy said, nodding confidently.

Next we needed to make the arm work. We got the arm to swing the way we wanted, but the ball kept rolling away—the arm was pushing it too hard.

Leila put her elbows on the table. "We need the ball to stay closer to her, or she won't get it through the maze."

Erin lowered her voice. "It's like Sammy and Sophia . . . he's trying to stay closer to her and—"

"OMG, stop, that's enough," I said, clapping my hand over her mouth. "We need to stay focused."

"I think we should try the help board," Maya said, blowing her bangs off her forehead. "Maybe someone could give us a good idea."

Lucy nodded. "Agreed."

Erin had the neatest handwriting in our group. On a bright yellow sticky note she wrote:

"We're having trouble not making the mechanical arm swing too much. Any ideas?"

She and Maya ran over to post it on the board. There were a lot of notes already on there.

When they got back, we heard an announcement for lunch. It felt a little weird to take a break when we'd been working so intensively, but I realized that my stomach was growling. There were tables set up on one side of the gym with big bowls of tossed salad and sandwich platters, drink dispensers filled with water and lemonade, and a dessert table with cake pops and cookies.

I saw Sammy just ahead of me in the food line, and as usual, I froze.

Maya was behind me. "Soph, you've gotta get over this. He's just a boy. Go talk to him!" She gave me a little shove, and I had no choice but to pick up a plate.

I cleared my throat. "Hey, Sammy."

Sammy turned around. "Oh, hey."

I started putting salad on my plate. "So . . . how's your robot going?"

"Pretty good. Yours?" he asked. We inched down the line.

"Still working on it." My brain decided to function properly for a second, and I remembered what he'd said at the water fountain the other day. I forced myself to talk instead of just standing there. "So, how's the secret part of your robot going?"

He smiled evasively at me as he took a chicken Caesar wrap. "*Really* well."

I was starting to get suspicious about their secret part.

"You know it has to be a module they have here, right?"

"Oh, it is." Sammy looked around, and then he lowered his voice. "I'll tell you this: There's no rule saying you have to use everything the way it was designed."

I raised my eyebrows in surprise. What could that mean?

We got our food and drinks and went outside. It was a really nice day, and kids were sitting on the ground eating lunch with their groups. Fatima's team was sprawled out on the lawn right next to mine, and Sammy's group was pretty close by, too. First we talked about our robots, but then we started talking about school. Fatima said she was helping plan the winter school dance at her school, and that got her and Maya started on themes. I could have sworn I saw Sammy glance at me during the talk about the dance, but I decided to ignore it. Like Tyson had said, if he wanted to ask me, he would. And if he didn't and I decided I wanted to go with him, I could always ask him myself, like Maya had mentioned.

After lunch, I thought about what Sammy had told me. Maybe he was right—not everything had to be used the way it was designed.

I had an idea about how to alter what Zahira's arm did, since it still didn't work. But it meant a pretty big change to our plan—the plan we'd spent *all* week working on—and I wasn't even sure it could work. I decided not to bring it up—at least not yet. Still, I played around with my idea on my computer for a bit.

Eventually Zahira was moving forward, and the button was working. But we still needed to solve the arm-ball problem *and* get Erin's dance music up and running, when we heard Mrs. Clark say, "Coding time's up!" She was in the center of the room, holding a microphone, and asked everyone to gather around her. Lucy, Erin, Leila, Maya, and I gave one another panicked looks.

"You'll have more time to code later, I promise," Mrs. Clark said, talking over the excited room of coders. "Taking breaks is an important part of coding and being creative—it gives your brain a chance to rest and rejuvenate itself."

She looked around. "And we have something fun planned for you!"

We put our modules down and gathered around Mrs. Clark. "And now for our very special activity...," she said suspensefully. "I'd like to introduce you all to Ms. Ana Kamat, chief technology officer of TechTown!"

Everyone clapped as Ms. Kamat joined Mrs. Clark. I noticed that the tables behind Mrs. Clark were now filled with tablets and smartphones instead of the modules for our robots.

"Thank you for the warm welcome!" Ms. Kamat said. "I'm so glad to be here, talking to all of you coders. I help create computers and computer programs at TechTown. Our mission is to build socially responsible technology that helps communities." She picked up a clipboard on a table next to her. "In fact, at TechTown, we have five new products coming out next year," she said. "And you will be the first to see them!"

Everyone started talking excitedly. Erin and I stood on our tiptoes to try and get a better look.

"I've brought examples of a few programs and gadgets. I'd love for you to try them out and tell me what you think." She looked over at Mrs. Clark. "As I'm sure you've learned in your coding clubs, a big part of developing programs, apps, and robots is getting feedback from users to figure out what works and what doesn't."

Ms. Kamat showed us a new system TechTown was releasing to help make sure water in small, rural areas was safe for animals and humans to drink, and a medical app that linked to the fitness tracker things we'd gotten in our TechTown backpacks.

Before we were allowed to explore, Ms. Kamat walked over to a three-foot-tall lump covered by a black cloth.

"And now, for the grand finale . . ."

Swoosh!

She pulled back the cloth dramatically, revealing a small robot. "Ta-da!" The robot had a white rounded plastic head and jointed arms and legs. My BFFs and I exchanged excited glances. It looked just like the robot Maya had designed for our Rockin' Robots T-shirts!

"This is a personal assistant bot we're testing at the local hospital. It can answer curious patients' questions about their conditions, and it can also complete simple commands, like 'Get me a glass of water.' It hasn't quite mastered things like open-heart surgery, but we're working on that."

Lucy leaned over to me and Leila and whispered, "This could totally be adapted to be the Babysitter 3000."

Leila smiled. "We should suggest she make it toothpaste-resistant."

"And don't forget peanut butter!" I added, chuckling.

"Keep in mind that none of these projects is final yet," Ms. Kamat explained as we went around the stations, checking everything out. "In fact, some of them, like our personal assistant bot, are still experimental. Sometimes you have to take a big risk to be innovative," Ms. Kamat continued. "But it's usually worth it. And if it still doesn't work, iterating—which is trying again and again—is a big part of computer science."

I smiled, but I was thinking about Zahira. Maybe it was worth telling my team about my idea to make her arm work better, even if it meant a big change. Like Ms. Kamat said, sometimes you have to take a big risk to make something better.

When we got back to our tables, I decided to go for it. "Listen, I have an idea for how we can fix Zahira's arm."

"Looks like Bradley did, too," Erin grumbled, showing me the green sticky note she'd pulled from the help board.

I read it out loud. "Glue the ball to the arm. Use chewing gum to attach the ball. Use Lucy's bracelet to tie the ball to the arm so it can't go far. You're welcome. B."

Lucy held out her arm with the special bracelet her mom

had given her. "He's hilarious," Lucy said wryly, rolling her eyes.

"Only in his own mind," Maya scoffed. "The bracelet thing is not happening." She paused. "Though we *could* use one of Erin's hair ties to tie the ball closer to the arm so it can't roll too far..."

"But that would mean taking off the speakers," Leila countered. "We can still only have four things, and I'm pretty sure a hair tie would count. If we could even use one."

"What was your idea, Soph?" Erin asked me, tightening her bun. "But know that I am down for giving you my hair tie if that's what we want to do."

I took a breath. "All the stuff Ms. Kamat showed us got me thinking—maybe we should change our plan," I said, watching my friends carefully.

No one looked thrilled with this idea.

I put my hands on the table. "You know how Ms. Kamat said sometimes you need to take a risk and make a change?" They all nodded. "I think we should forget the ball and put in an LED light instead."

"But I thought you liked the ball part," Erin challenged, frowning.

"And we already programmed the arm," Leila reminded me.

"I do like the ball part," I said. "And we can leave the arm the way it is. I just don't think the ball part is working, and Zahira won't be able to get through the maze if she's chasing the ball that far, right?"

They all nodded again.

"All I'm saying is, maybe we try something different."

"But then what would the arm do?" Lucy asked. "It's got to have a purpose."

"Could it ... dance?" I suggested, thinking out loud.

"Dance?" Maya repeated.

"I thought you didn't like that idea," Erin said.

"Well, I didn't think it was possible," I explained, lifting Zahira's arm. "But maybe I underestimated Zahira."

"If you're thinking she can do the sprinkler, stop right now," Lucy said.

Erin rubbed her chin thoughtfully. "I can't really see her doing the shopping cart, either, but ..."

I shook my head so hard, my hair brushed Erin and Lucy's cheeks. "No, no, no!" They all gave me confused looks. "Instead of the arm pushing the ball through, we have lights blink, music play, and an arm that dances to the beat of Erin's song!"

A hush fell over my friends. I could tell they were trying to picture my idea.

"That's actually pretty funny," Erin finally admitted. "This could work!"

I smiled. "Sammy said we don't have to use everything the way it was originally supposed to be used."

"Oooh, Sammy!" Maya nudged Lucy.

I gave her a stern look. "Don't even start."

I started typing on my keyboard and pointed to a spot on the screen. "We can change the coding here." I pointed to another line. "And here."

Maya and Lucy raced to the supply table to exchange the ball and came back with an LED light board.

After we'd made the changes and plugged in the LED light board to Zahira's motherboard, I uploaded the music to the robot's motherboard and set the coding in motion. Zahira's arm wiggled in all directions to the music, which played in a loop. The lights flashed red, green, and blue, but not to the beat at all. She looked totally silly. But there was no doubt about it: She was dancing!

"OMG, I saw Bradley at a bar mitzvah last month, and that's exactly how he moved on the dance floor!" Maya squealed, cracking us up.

"You're terrible," Leila said, shaking her head, but she was laughing.

"Looks like I've got some real competition," Erin said.

She began doing her silly robot dance.

"Excuse me!" A short kid with braces came running over to us. "I know we're supposed to go to the board, but you guys look like you know what you're doing, and we're running out of time. Our robot keeps hitting the wall, and we can't figure it out. Can you help us?"

"Um, sure," Leila said as we all nodded. "Guys, I'll be back." She and the kid raced off.

"I love how helpful everyone is here," Maya said as we watched the two teams next to us give each other advice.

"Yeah," I said. It was a pretty cool atmosphere.

Before we knew it, it was time for Zahira to do a practice run through the maze.

"Where's Leila?" Lucy asked, scanning the room. We had some time . . . but not much. We waited patiently, watching other teams send their robots through. There were some really cool ones: a robot that carried blocks in the bulldozer arm and dumped them at the finish line, one that unwound a ball of string behind it to show its path, and one that had a spinning propeller on top—though I couldn't figure out why it was there or what it did.

"I'm back," Leila gasped, running up to us. "They just needed to use sensors."

"Phew," Erin said, scooting over so Leila could squeeze in next to her.

I noticed that Bradley and Sammy's team wasn't coming over to practice. Maybe they thought they didn't need to practice . . . or maybe they still wanted to keep what their robot did a secret. I realized that maybe that was a good idea—we didn't want everyone to know what Zahira was going to do before the actual maze run.

"We should keep Zahira's dancing a secret," I whispered to my friends, glancing over my shoulder at Sammy. "Let's just try the sensors and the movement through the maze," I told them.

"Good idea," Erin said. "That's the hardest part, anyway."

Maya had walked up to the maze and waved her hand at us, calling us over. "It's our turn."

I headed to the starting line and squatted down, setting Zahira on the green arrow at the start of the maze. "Time to see what you can do, Zahira . . . ," I whispered to her.

Ms. Kamat was running the practices. "Go!" she said, and blew a whistle.

Erin dashed back to the computer and clicked "run" on our program.

Zahira crossed the starting line, just like she was supposed to. When she hit the first wall, she sensed it and turned left. We all looked at one another and grinned. Then she turned left again to an opening in the maze, where she moved forward one more time.

"Zahira! Zahira!" Lucy and Maya were whooping and yelling.

"It works!" Leila shouted over to where Erin sat. "She actually works!"

At the next wall, Zahira turned left. But then she went left again ... and again ... and again.

I gasped. "Oh no!"

"Looks like you girls have a problem," Ms. Kamat said as Zahira continued to turn in circles. "Can you try to solve it?"

Erin looked over at us, a panicky look on her face. "I don't know what to do!" she called to us.

I could tell Ms. Kamat wasn't going to help—it was up to us. With a deep breath, I scooped up Zahira, cradled her in my arms, and joined my friends on the sidelines.

Erin took her hands off the keyboard and held her hands up in a shrug. "I have no idea how to fix this."

"Let's look at our plan again," Maya said, already heading back to her computer.

"No, Maya, there's not enough time," I argued, stopping her. "And we already changed it once. I think we should try to fix the code until Zahira works."

"And we've already worked on the plan so much," Leila said. "I don't think that's where the problem is. Sophia's right. We don't want to make things worse. Let's go through the code again."

"Okay, fine," Maya gave in. "I guess you're right. I mean, I'd hate to fix the way she moves but then mess up the arm or lights."

"True," Lucy said. "Let's go over it all, line by line. We'll figure this out!"

We were about to rush back to our table when I noticed Ms. Kamat looking at us. She was close enough to have heard our entire conversation, but I couldn't tell what she was thinking.

Was there any way we could get Zahira to finish the maze? We'd put so much work into her—and I didn't want Sammy's robot to beat us.

But we were running out of time.

Chapter Eleven

"It's the left turn!" I exclaimed after we looked through the code a few times. "That's the issue. Zahira only knows how to go left!"

"Five minutes left!" Ms. Kamat announced.

I could see the judges gathering near the maze. Students were already carrying their projects over.

In the end, we made a few changes to the code but didn't have time to think through whether it was right or not. We figured anything was worth a try.

"Time's up!" Mrs. Clark called the last straggling teams to the maze. "If you're visiting, please take your seats. And hackathon participants, please put your team T-shirts on for the final maze runs."

I hadn't even noticed, but some visitors had gathered around the maze. Lucy's parents and Leila's little brother waved at us. I thought about my mom not being there and got a bit sad, but then I remembered that at least I'd been able to come to the hackathon—thanks to my friends.

We all got our T-shirts and put them on. Suddenly it felt real. We were about to compete!

And then, far out in the crowd, I spotted Abuela sneaking into the community center. She saw me and started waving frantically. I couldn't believe it! She must have come back early from Marissa's to see me. I felt a rush of happiness and waved back with a huge grin.

"We'll go in order of your table station numbers," Mrs. Clark told the groups. "Table one."

The first group that went had a basic robot. They directed it by remote control and had no extra modules. It only went through the maze, and pretty slowly at that.

Another group had their robot drag the ball behind it with a string rope. And the group that had asked Leila for advice used sensors to detect distance and avoid the walls.

"They owe you," Lucy whispered in Leila's ear.

Leila shrugged. "They were really nice. I'm glad I could help them."

Machine Madness was up next.

"Looking forward to your surprise," I called over to Sammy as he walked past me to the starting line.

"We're going to beat all speed records for doing a maze," Bradley said, strutting forward with a cocky grin. "Any maze. Ever."

Maya rolled her eyes. "Good luck with that."

Machine Madness gave one another a round of high fives while Alicia put their robot on the start line. Their robot had a huge swinging arm, just like Zahira did.

"Okay, go!" Ms. Kamat said, and blew her whistle.

The robot gripped a block in its arm until it reached the first wall. But instead of turning left or right or even backing up, it put the block down. Then, using its arm, it lifted itself onto the block and over the wall. Once on the other side, it turned back and reached over the wall with its arm to collect the block. Then it moved on to the next wall and did the whole thing over again. After going over two walls, all the robot had left to do was move straight to the finish line. I had to admit, it was pretty creative—and efficient.

"That was fast!" Ms. Kamat said, checking the time and making a note on her clipboard. "First place so far."

Bradley and Sammy started dancing.

"And the most innovative, as well," Ms. Kamat added.

"Isn't that cheating?" Erin asked Ms. Kamat, saying what we all were thinking. "I mean, they went over the maze instead of through it."

Ms. Kamat flipped a few pages on her clipboard. "Well, it's certainly not the way we expected the robot to finish the maze, but the rules don't say anything against going over."

"The time stands," another judge announced. "Machine Madness has the score to beat!"

"There's no way we can top that," Maya said darkly. We'd worked so hard, and now we weren't even sure our robot would travel past the first wall.

I looked at my friends. "We did our best," I said, channeling Coach Tilton. "Time to leave it all on the field. No holding back."

"Rockin' Robots!" Ms. Kamat called our group. "You're up!"

"Let's see this robot rock," Erin said, sounding determined. I set Zahira down at the beginning of the maze, and Erin initiated the code on her laptop.

At the starting line, Zahira's lights began blinking constantly. Soon after, Erin's song started playing from the speakers we'd attached to the rover. Then Zahira's arm began to swing, and it almost seemed like she was trying to move to the rhythm of the song.

She started through the maze perfectly. She moved forward to the first wall, sensed it like she was supposed to . . . and then, just when she was supposed to turn, she began to spin. She kept going left, left, and left, but it was happening so fast that it seemed like she was spinning.

"She's only going left!" Lucy said, sounding panicked. And on top of that, her arm was swinging wildly, with the music still playing.

"Yeah, but why?" Erin asked, her hands on her head.

I was horrified by what was happening. I looked over at Ms. Kamat, but to my surprise, she was chuckling. Maya looked over at me and started laughing.

"It really looks like Zahira's dancing!" she said.

We all realized how ridiculous Zahira looked and cracked up together. Then other kids and some of the visitors started laughing, too. Even Mrs. Clark was giggling.

Zahira might not be able to pass the first part of the maze, but she sure could bust some moves!

Erin turned up the music, and we all began to dance, swinging our arms like Zahira. Pretty soon, the whole room was dancing along to Erin's song and Zahira's funky moves. It didn't matter anymore that Zahira had failed miserably at getting through the maze—we'd started the most *epic* robot dance party!

After the dance party (and Zahira's coming in last,

since she didn't even make it through the maze) we were cleaning up at our table when Ms. Kamat came over to us.

"Hi, girls," she said. "I know your robot didn't work how you expected. But I was impressed at your problem-solving style."

"Thanks," I said, unplugging Zahira's arm. "I'm not sure we have much of a problem-solving style, though. Zahira didn't exactly do what we planned."

"Yeah, she was supposed to move her arms like she was dancing, not turn around nonstop!" Erin said, sighing.

"I know," Ms. Kamat answered. "But some problems take more time than we had here." She looked at our robot. "Have you girls learned about feature creep yet?" We shook our heads. "It's when you put too many things in a computer program—or robot, in this case—and it can't do any of them exactly as intended. Too many features creep in."

I laughed. "Well, that's definitely what happened to Zahira!"

"Indeed," Ms. Kamat continued. "There's always so much to learn with computer programming." She reached into her tote bag and pulled out a card. "I know you didn't win a prize, but I still have an offer."

We all stopped cleaning up for a minute.

"I heard you trying to figure out why your robot would only go left." She handed me the business card. "Most kids would have gone back and started rethinking their whole plan, potentially making things worse in the process."

"Ha! We considered that," Maya said.

"I know." Ms. Kamat nodded. "But in the end you decided to review your original concept, to determine where things had gone wrong." She looked at each of us in turn, her eyes finally resting on me. "That was impressive."

"Thanks," I said, feeling flattered.

"Computer programing is all about creativity, grit, and teamwork, and you girls showed today that you have all of that, so I want you to see what else you can do with it." She pointed at her business card. "I'd like to invite you all to come to TechTown for a personal tour. I'd love to show you around." She leaned in toward us and whispered, "I might even have a prototype drone to show off."

My friends and I all looked at one another in amazement and grinned.

All I'd wanted to do was beat everyone else in the hackathon. But now I didn't even care that Zahira hadn't made it through the maze—or that we had (technically) lost. Because with what Ms. Kamat had just told the Rockin' Robots, we were winners all the way.

Chapter Twelve

$\mathcal{A}$fter the dance party and cleanup, it was finally time to go home. Abuela had found me after the maze runs and gushed about how hackathons were the most fun thing ever—she even said she might want to participate in one. I tried to explain that they probably didn't all end in dance extravaganzas.

"Well, maybe they should," she'd said firmly as I waved goodbye. Ellie's grandmother overheard our conversation, and soon she and Abuela were chatting away about learning to code and taking a flamenco dance class together at the Y.

"That was the *best* dance party!" Leila declared as we headed out of the community center. She was carrying Zahira.

"Like we're the *best* group!" Maya said.

"And today was the *best* hackathon!" Erin added.

I started to say "We are the *best*—" when Lucy cut in.

"*Best* friends," she finished.

"You guys *are* the best," I gushed.

"Talking about us again?" It was Bradley. "We still have the *best* robot," Bradley bragged as he, Sammy, Alicia, and Ellie came walking up next to us. Bradley held out their team's robot. "We're calling him the Climb Over Rover."

Their robot had placed pretty high, though the winner was a robot from another school that sped through the maze tipped on two wheels. I still wasn't sure how they'd managed to do that. It was pretty epic.

"We won a pizza party from that new place near school," Bradley said smugly.

While Bradley and the others discussed the pizza party, Sammy stepped up next to me. "Hey," he whispered. "Can I talk to you?"

We started walking a bit slower, falling behind the others.

"What's up?" I asked, trying to act calm.

Sammy looked down at the ground. "So, you know . . . the dance?" He shuffled his feet around.

I thought about what Tyson and Maya had said. I realized that I kind of did want to go to the dance with

Sammy, and it seemed like he wanted to, also.

I took a deep breath. "You want to go together?" I couldn't believe those words had just come out of my mouth.

Sammy looked up at me wide-eyed and then broke into a grin. "That'd be awesome." He reached for my hand. I let him take it, even though it was a sweaty mess—but his was, too. Right before we reached the others, he let go of my hand and looked at me with his warm, dark eyes. "Text you later?"

"Okay." I nodded, my heart racing.

Sammy's mom was giving his team rides home, and Lucy's dad was going to drive us to her house—he'd just stopped to talk to another parent inside. We'd all planned to hang out at Lucy's for a while before going home.

As soon as I caught up with my friends, they pounced. "What was *that* about?" Lucy shrieked as she and Maya, Erin, and Leila crowded around me.

I touched my hot cheeks. "I asked Sammy to the dance!" I exclaimed, surprising even myself.

"You *didn't*!" Maya said, hitting me on the arm. "What did you say?"

"I just asked him to go with me!" I was feeling pretty proud of myself.

"That's so cool!" Leila said.

Erin hugged me. "You're awesome."

"Okay, but you have to promise not to wear raggedy sports shirts or sweatpants," Maya said, scanning my outfit with her finger.

I put my hands over my heart. "Promise."

I looked at my friends and thought how I wouldn't be here if it weren't for them helping me out that morning. And if I wasn't here, I wouldn't have been able to help code Zahira's amazing dance moves. And ask Sammy to the dance.

"Smile!" Erin held her phone up, and we threw our arms around one another and made silly faces, making sure to hold Zahira up high.

"Text it to all of us," Maya said.

"Done." Erin nodded, tapping her phone.

I pulled out my phone and looked at the picture that popped up on my screen. "Rockin' Robots forever," I said, waves of happiness washing over me. Not only did I have the absolute *best*, most epic team . . . I had the absolute best BFFs.

Acknowledgments

Thank you to Sophie Courtney, Matt Cohen, Yoni Cohen, Jonah Lerner, and Laura Sebastian. And thanks to the girls who invited me to their hackathon and shared their programs. Plus, I was lucky to get some special advice from the tween girls at Camp Stein, Cabin Namer 2016!

Don't miss these other Girls Who Code books!